HER CONVICT WOLF

OBSESSED MATES BOOK 6

ARIANA HAWKES

Copyright ©2023 by Ariana Hawkes

All rights reserved. No part of this publication may be reproduced, distributed, or transmitted in any form or by any means, including photocopying, recording, or other electronic or mechanical methods, without the prior written permission of the publisher, except in the case of brief quotations embodied in critical reviews and certain other noncommercial uses permitted by copyright law.

This is a work of fiction. Names, characters, businesses, places, events and incidents are either the products of the author's imagination or used in a fictitious manner. Any resemblance to actual persons, living or dead, or actual events and businesses is purely coincidental.

Imprint: Independently published

ISBN: 9798866370733

Cover art: Thunderface Design

www.arianahawkes.com

CONTENTS

Chapter 1	1
Chapter 2	14
Chapter 3	19
Chapter 4	31
Chapter 5	39
Chapter 6	50
Chapter 7	59
Chapter 8	67
Chapter 9	72
Chapter 10	85
Chapter 11	95
Chapter 12	105
Chapter 13	113
Epilogue	118
Epilogue	121
Read the other books in the series	129
Read my Obsessed Mountain Mates series	131
Read the rest of my catalogue	133
My other matchmaking series	135
Connect with me	137
Get two free books	139
Reading guide to all of my books	141

1

Emory

Oookay… I skip from one cooking pot to another, stirring like a whirlwind. Everything is under control. I've got six pots bubbling on two stoves; a lasagna and a tray bake in the oven, and I've just finished making up and wrapping a bunch of bologna and provolone sandwiches.

I told my boss I could do thirty extra lunches today, and I've pulled it off.

I take a moment to wipe a bunch of steam off my glasses and survey my work.

Running a kitchen used to be my dream—well, before I grew up and understood the life I'd been born into—and I am a little bit proud of myself for putting all this together. In my fantasies, I'd have my very own restaurant, and a whole team behind me, chorusing "yes, chef!" to my every command. But right now, I'll settle for cooking lunches for convicts.

I hold my glasses up to the light, then I put them back on. Like my dark-brown contact lenses, they're non-prescription, and they're necessary. Along with my dyed red hair, piercings and ultra-realistic fake tattoos, they make me unrecognizable as the girl I used to be.

"Tiana! How you doing, hun?" The kitchen door swings open and Meredith, my boss, bustles in.

My name is not Tiana. And I hate that I've given my kind-hearted boss a fake name, but it's also necessary.

I've built a little life for myself in Perdue Town—this little sanctuary of the lost. I don't feel totally safe here—and I probably never will—but since I've been hiding out here, working in the kitchen of Sinner's Refuge, I've stopped feeling like some terrified prey animal, just waiting to be devoured.

"Good—I think," I reply, stirring four pots in quick succession.

Meredith stops in the middle of the kitchen, raises her nose and sniffs hard. Then she narrows her eyes at me. "Tiana, are you cooking *fancy* food again?"

I giggle. "I just added a couple of herbs and spices," I admit.

"Well, it smells fantastic. Hope you'll have a couple of portions left over for staff?"

"Already assigned," I tell her happily.

"Will you be ready for eleven-forty-five pick up?"

"Yup. Sure will."

She squeezes my shoulder. "Well done, hun. You're doing great."

This morning, Meredith got a call from the federal prison service, asking if we'd be willing to provide thirty lunches for a convict chain gang. They're working on a highway twenty minutes from here, and their usual catering company let them down.

"Sure thing," I told her right away. I'm by myself in the kitchen at the moment—since her sister, who usually works here, is out of town for the next few days—but I was excited by the challenge. Besides, I don't want to refuse Meredith anything. She's been so good to me.

She told me to focus on quantity rather than quality, because the prisoners will be ravenous after laboring in the hot sun all morning. But I want to make sure they enjoy their food. If the TV shows are anything to go by, prison food is one step up from pig slop. I know some of these men must've done terrible things. But others might have been wrongfully convicted. Or they were just in the wrong place at the wrong time. I know about that more than most. And I'll be glad if I can make their day a little brighter.

I keep an eye on the clock, and at eleven-thirty a.m., I start ladling all the food into delivery cartons. By eleven forty-five, I'm all done, everything packed up and labeled.

But Meredith is nowhere to be seen. Maybe the bar got busy.

While I'm waiting on her, I make sure everything is ready for the pub's regular lunchtime rush.

At eleven fifty-three, she bursts into the kitchen. "The darn delivery company screwed us over!"

"What?"

"They're not coming. They're not allowed to expose their drivers to unreasonable danger, yada yada…" She rolls her eyes. "I don't know whether they're referring to Perdue or to the convicts. But the upshot is, they're not coming, and we have no way of getting the prisoners' lunches to them."

I turn and stare at all the packed-up cartons in dismay. "B-but all the prisoners will go hungry."

Meredith's expression softens. "You're the sweetest person, Tiana. There was me thinking of all the food going to waste. But yes, there are going to be a bunch of empty convict bellies, too." She exhales slowly and gives me a long look. "I hate to ask you this, hun. I know you're not keen on going outside and all…"

Oh no.

My gut tightens. I know what's coming.

"…Is there any chance you'd be willing to drive these over yourself?"

My stomach flips and I think I'm going to be sick. I avoid leaving my little safety triangle of bar, apartment and supermarket. Everyone here knows it, and I've let them think I'm agoraphobic. And yes, I am scared shitless of the outdoors. But it's not a phobia—it's a legitimate fear. There are people out there who would kill me without thinking twice. Some of them I've known all my life. And I've got reason to think they're actively looking for me.

I'm not naïve enough to think that no one can get to me here, but at least I know every shadow, every alleyway. Every corner where someone could surprise me.

The last thing I want to do is step outside this comfort zone I've created. But if I don't, the convicts won't eat, and Meredith won't get paid for all this food.

Crap. Crap. Crap.

"Okay, I'll do it," I hear myself saying.

She beams. "You can be real quick. Just hand the food over to the guards, and zip right back here."

"Sure thing," I mumble. My underarms already feel damp.

This doesn't have to be a big deal, I tell myself, while Meredith and I pack all the cartons into the trunk and backseats of my crappy old car. I'm not going to run into anyone I know. And even if I do, they won't recognize me. In the last year, I've gone from being a blonde, blue-eyed picture of innocence, to a hip, flame-haired chick with dark, doe eyes. The girl I used to be would never have styled herself like that. I've even gotten curves, from all the good food I've been eating here.

"Thank you, Ti. Means a lot." Meredith presses a hand to her heart.

I bend my lips into a smile. It's the right thing to do.

And I'll be back soon.

* * *

IT'S A BLISTERING HOT DAY, a heat haze shimmering over the highway as I drive north from Perdue.

With every mile, my stomach turns another notch. *It's fine,* I tell myself over and over. *You'll be in and out in five minutes, just like Meredith said.*

Twenty minutes later, I spot a cluster of orange off

to the side of the highway. The convicts! My heart beats faster. But they look like they're hidden in a dust cloud. As I draw closer, I see why. They're breaking rocks. Like something from a bygone era, they're hacking at a massive chunk of rock with pickaxes. In ninety-five-degree heat.

I pull into a makeshift parking lot beside a long gray van with tiny windows. When I climb out of my car, a wall of heat hits me. It's like opening an oven door right in your face.

Heads turn in my direction, and I realize that I'm the only woman amid this mass of testosterone.

The prisoners are massive, scary-looking guys, working bareheaded, their skin streaked with dirt and perspiration. They're shackled to each other by their wrists and ankles, while a bunch of prison guards are training firearms on them.

"Where shall I unload the food?" I call to the nearest guard. He's leaning against the van in a patch of shade.

He pulls his sunglasses down. "There's a table right *there*." He has a slow, whiny-sounding voice. I see where he's pointing and open the trunk. The heat bears down on me as I ferry the cartons over to the table. *Sheesh.* Sweat trickles down the sides of my face and I feel my cheeks getting hot.

When I see that the convicts are breaking for lunch, I hurry to finish before they arrive. The guards are waving their guns at them and screaming at them to leave their tools behind.

"Do they have to threaten them like that?" I ask the

guard, who's been watching me the whole time, chewing on a grass stalk.

He grins at me, the stalk poking out between his teeth. "*Yew* don't know them, miss." He scans me from head to toe, before his gaze comes to rest on my tits. I don't care. I'm wearing a push-up bra as part of my disguise.

"They'd snap your spine soon as look at you. That one"—he points at the prisoner at the head of the chain gang—"murdered three women. Because he was bored."

The prisoner looks feral. Crazed eyes, heavily scarred skin, tattoos covering his shaven head. When he notices our attention on him, he grins, revealing dark, glittering teeth.

I gulp. "They've all done stuff like that?"

"Pretty much. Rape, murder. Torture. *Yew* name it." He cackles. He's enjoying this.

As I scan them, my attention zones in on one in the middle of the line. He's taller than the rest. Massive shoulders. Dark hair. His face is smeared with dirt, but a strange light glows from his eyes.

There's something magnetic about him.

Like he's calling to me.

Calling? What?

I don't know where that thought came from. But now it's planted itself in my brain, I can't get rid of it.

I'm no longer aware of anything else—the heat, the danger, the prisoners and guards. All my attention, my senses are focused on him.

And *holy crap*, he's looking at me, too. He's at least thirty yards away, but I can literally feel his attention on me. The hairs on my forearms are standing on end and shivers run through my body.

"How about that one?" I don't really want to ask the question, but I have to know. "The big guy in the middle."

"That one—?" The guard sounds disappointed. "I dunno. It's classified. But something *real* bad I reckon. They keep him in an electric cage at night."

An *electric cage*? Bars and chains aren't enough to contain him? I try to cast a discreet glance at him, but he's still watching me. He's standing very still, and I feel like his eyes are boring right into me. Like he can see through my disguise. See what I look like under my clothes. My cheeks burn even hotter.

Is he a shifter? He reminds me of the guys who come into the pub—half man, half beast, with fierce eyes and gruff ways.

The first convict approaches the table. He's gnashing his teeth and snorting like a rabid beast.

"Okay, I'll be off now," I squeak.

"Oh, no, sweetcheeks. *Yew* gotta serve 'em, too," the guard whines.

"No, that's not part of it. I'm just doing delivery. We're a restaurant, not a catering service."

He shakes his head sadly. "We're not allowed to serve them. Prison protocol. It disrupts the power balance."

I snort. "Better if an unarmed civilian serves them instead?"

"Up to you," he says in a sing-song voice. *"Yew* don't feed them, they don't *eat*."

Fuck.

Each one of them looks like he could tear my head off with his teeth. The thought of being in arms' reach of them fills me with terror.

Definitely not what I signed up for. This situation is getting worse and worse.

"Go on, miss, they won't hurt you. We'll have guns trained on them at all times."

I puff out my cheeks. I hate that this asshole is putting me in this position. But I also hate the thought that the prisoners will go hungry. I calculate. There are thirty of them. If each one takes thirty seconds to serve, I'll be done in fifteen minutes. Then I'll be back in my car and straight back to Perdue.

I take a deep breath.

"Okay," I say.

My heart hammers as the first convict approaches. His nostrils are twitching ravenously.

"I've got beef stew. Chicken tray bake—"

"Food!!" he roars.

"F-food, right." My hands shake as I shove a bunch of cartons at him.

He snatches them, tears the lid off the first one, and starts shoveling beef stew into his mouth with his hands.

"Get a move on, prisoner." One of the guards jabs him in the back with the butt of his gun. He lets out a roar of rage, but keeps eating.

I wind up giving each convict a portion of everything. I'm so glad I made a ton of food. Each guy is as feral as the last, but from the sounds they're making as they eat, I can tell they're enjoying it. And I'm glad.

Ten guys done. Ten more minutes until I'll be out of here.

It can't come soon enough. The back of my shirt is clinging to my back and perspiration is stinging my eyes.

When the eleventh prisoner snatches up the cartons with a grunt, my heart beats faster.

Because the next guy is the extra-huge one. The one whose eyes have been burning into me this entire time.

The guard prods him with his rifle, directing him in front of me. My mouth has gone extra dry. I keep my head down, just shove the food at him.

"Beef and chicken, please," says a deep baritone voice.

That's not the voice of a beast.

My head snaps up.

It's a sexy voice. A voice that does things to me. Sends tingles from my core to my nipples and back again.

Oh, god. And now I'm looking right into his eyes. They're piercing blue; light irises ringed with black. Thick lashes, heavy black brows.

And they're filling with recognition.

My breath hitches.

No. Not possible.

But now I'm hyperventilating, because there's something familiar about him, too.

Who is he?

The reality is, there are so many people he could be. My father always had a ton of associates coming over to the house.

Now, one of them's in jail. Not a massive shocker, since all my father's associates were criminals.

Stay calm. Breathe and pass him his food. I drop my gaze again, thrust the chicken, beef, and a bologna sandwich at him.

"Wait—" His voice again.

I look up. I can't help it.

Torment burns in his eyes. He opens his mouth to say more—

The guard jabs his rifle into his kidney. He grunts, and I flinch. It's vicious; way excessive. Two more guards cock their rifles at his head, step in closer.

He doesn't move. He just stands there looking furious.

He sleeps in an electric cage.

The thought sizzles, white hot in my brain.

Who is he? Why is he having this effect on me?

He gives me one more burning look, then another convict takes his place.

Blood pounds in my ears. I count each prisoner off, shoving the food cartons at them like an automaton. Breathing in and out.

No big deal... no big deal...

Prisoner twenty-six… twenty-seven. I'll be out of here in three minutes.

I will not look at him again.

I'll forget I ever saw him.

I picture myself getting back in my car, hightailing it back to Perdue. Hiding out in the pub kitchen. Keeping myself safe from prying eyes. I'll happily spend the rest of my life like that—

Roarrr!!! An incredible sound rips through the air. I jerk away from the table, spin around. At the far end of the chain gang, two of the prisoners are beating the hell out of each other. Bellows and screams; a sickening thud as one headbutts the other. And then a bunch more of them pile in. Fists pounding, chains flying.

"Fucking hell!" screams a guard. "Shoot 'em… in the leg!" They charge off, rifles cocked.

I stand, rooted to the spot. *Run, run, run!* My brain is screaming.

There's a bang, and another one. *Yikes.* I throw myself flat on the ground, cover my face.

But between my fingers, I see a blur of orange breaking away from the rest.

Oh, my god. One of the prisoners has escaped.

And he's coming right for me.

It's him.

The earth shakes as he charges toward me. A mass of muscle and raw energy.

He bounds to a stop, inches away, and crouches down in front of me. His chains are hanging loose on his arms and legs and his eyes are blazing.

Whimper escapes my lips. Is he going to tear my throat out with his bare hands?

"Emory!" he grates out.

I'm going to be sick. "Not Emory," I croak, but it's way too late for that.

"Emory, it's Maxim," he urges, eyes burning with frustration.

Maxim. His name hurtles back through the years. My father's bodyguard. From a long, long time ago.

"W-why are you here, in jail?" I stammer.

Those glowing eyes of his narrow as they flick from my glasses to my hair, to the tattoo creeping up from the neckline of my shirt. "You're in hiding. But you're not safe here. You need to—"

"Fuck...that motherfucker's escaped!" a guard bawls. "Shoot!"

There's a clicking sound, followed by a gunshot.

"Agghh!" Maxim grabs his shoulder. Blood spatters between his fingers.

"Maxim! Oh, my god!" I scream.

They shot him. They fucking shot him.

I stay flat on the ground, head swiveling. There are guns pointing everywhere. Mean, trigger-happy guards, who look about ready to kill everyone in sight.

"You need to get the hell out of here, miss!" one of the guards screams. His eyes are bugged out; he looks high. "Forget this ever happened."

"Go! I'll come back for you," Maxim grunts, features drawn with pain.

What does he mean? I barely have time to think as I give him one more panicked glance, then I get up and *run like hell.*

2

Maxim

I charge up and down my cell, fists bunched, jaw clenched, bouncing off the bars. They hum and crackle, sending searing volts through me, but I hardly notice. I'm struggling to keep my beast inside. Its fur keeps bursting through my skin. I'm bruised and bleeding in a bunch of places, and the open wound in my shoulder is smarting. They didn't stitch it up. Guess I'm lucky they dug the bullet out at all. Would've been a bitch doing it by myself.

I don't give a shit about that anyway.

All I care about is Emory.

My ex-boss's little girl. I haven't seen her for ten years at least. She was just a kid the last time I saw her. Blonde, blue-eyed and cute as a button. When she was real small, she was fearless. She wasn't scared of me, like most people were. She used to like using me as a climbing frame. I'd swing her around and around, let her stand on my shoulders. I remember thinking, I wish she could stay as a kid forever, so she'd never find out who her father really was.

But by the time she was around ten, she'd become watchful. She was starting to figure out the world she belonged to. And it made my heart ache, and I wanted to protect her from all that. But what could I do? I was just an employee. Then her father fired me, and she was out of reach behind tall gates and heavy guard.

The Emory I saw today is nothing like that little girl. Every last thing about her appearance is different. Even her eyes have changed color, somehow. And she's gotten so beautiful. She used to be such a little tomboy. It never occurred to me that she'd grow up to be such an attractive woman. Those lush lips. Those killer curves. I even like her tattoos. Never been a guy for body art, but I can't stop wondering where the ink on her chest finishes up. The thought of her naked is driving my beast crazy. She's a beautiful, ripe peach, just waiting to be claimed.

Damn. I shouldn't be thinking about her that way. She's also a good fifteen years younger than me.

And she's in a ton of danger.

What I need to focus on is protecting her.

How the hell has she wound up delivering lunches to a bunch of feral convicts?

She's broken away from her family, that much is obvious.

Her father is in jail. The rumors run like wildfire in our prison network. People say he's thinking of turning.

Everyone who's affiliated to him in any way is in big trouble right now.

She probably thinks her disguise is enough. But she's dead wrong.

She's not safe. Either from her family, or their ex-associates.

I hated leaving her behind today. But here I am, caged like a beast by the federal prison service. And for good reason. My younger brother, Travis, has been in jail for the past five years. Not a human jail like this one, but a max-security, top-secret shifter prison. He got screwed with a whole life sentence for a murder he didn't commit. But I've done a deal with the DA. This place is as corrupt as hell. They wanted someone on the inside to gather intel on the mob and the guards who are running it. So, I've gone undercover. If I help them out, they'll release him. I've gotten a ton of evidence and I'm almost there—

Need to get to Emory!

My beast's claws rip through the ends of my fingers. It wraps its paws around the bars and shakes them. Electric shocks vibrate through my body. But I hold on. The pain helps me focus.

"Keep the fucking noise down, prisoner!" bawls one of the guards. One of the pricks who beat me with a baton today. I clench my teeth, biting back a torrent of rage. I could snap his neck with my little finger. And I'd do it with pleasure. But I need to keep my cover.

There's a big event happening in three days' time.

Human trafficking. If it all goes according to plan, I'll have all the evidence I need to trade for Travis's freedom.

But Emory needs me now.

Every minute she's alone is a risk to her safety.

I've got to protect her.

I close my eyes, remembering the last time I saw her. Her father's security team was marching me off the premises. Fired for some crazy bullshit. But I broke away from them. Looked for her until I found her, up in her treehouse. I explained that I was going away, and she burst into tears. She'd already lost her mama, poor little thing, and her father was an asshole, obviously. She was lonely. I think that was why she'd sought me out for friendship. I gave her a little plush rabbit. She was too old for it really, but I'd bought it on impulse, and I'd been planning to give it to her on her birthday.

"When are you coming back?" she wailed.

"Someday," I told her. What a lie. I was never allowed back in the compound. And my life moved on in other directions. I built my own multi-million-dollar security company. Fought like hell to make it happen.

Now, fate has given me a second chance to help her.

My beast roars. *Find her!*

But my brother…

He's been rotting in jail all these years. This is my one chance to help him. I've already been in this place for six months, keeping my cover, despite the fact I'm so much bigger and stronger than these poor human fuckers. Just three more days and I can get him out…

Fuck. Fuck. Fuck.

I grab at the bars. Electricity pours through my body in agonizing vibrations. I tense my muscles. The bars start to bend. An alarm goes off—

3

Emory

I turn all the locks and bolts on my apartment door. Then I walk into my kitchen, flick on the kettle, and collapse onto a chair.

Now I'm alone, it all washes over me.

My father's old bodyguard is in jail. And he got shot. Because of me.

It was so awful. When I looked in the rearview mirror, right before I screeched onto the highway, he was facedown in the dirt, a bunch of guards beating on him with batons.

Please let him be okay.

I still can't get my head around what he did. He managed to break out of those heavy chains, and got himself shot because he needed to warn me…

His words bounce around my head.

You're not safe here.

But how does he know?

And what's he doing in a jail for dangerous prisoners?

I get up to make the tea, then I pace up and down, arms wrapped around my body.

He said he's coming back for me. But how, when he's locked up in a high security prison?

And what am I to him anyway?

Just his ex-employer's little daughter.

Maxim was so kind to me when I was small.

I remember I used to clamber all over him, and he'd just sit there, like a tree, and let me do it. And when I was older, he built me a treehouse. He used to work on it when he was off shift. He made it real nice and cozy, with a little table and a set of chairs to entertain my friends. I didn't have any real friends in those days—there were no other kids in the complex—but he always talked to my stuffed animals like they were my friends. I'd invite him to tea parties, and he'd sit on the little platform, cross-legged, his huge bulk taking up half the space, pretending to drink from a tiny teacup.

Then one day, he left. He told me he was going on a long vacation. For a while, I was hurt. I thought he'd abandoned me, and I cried myself to sleep at night. But when I got older, I realized my father had fired him.

The one person in my life who'd cared for me.

I actually used to have a little-kid crush on him. Suddenly, I'm smiling at the memory. He was kinda scary-looking—so huge, with a broad, hard face and fierce eyes—but I used to think he looked real handsome in the sharp suit he wore when he was on duty. And I think I may have asked him if he'd marry me.

Gosh, how embarrassing. Hopefully he's forgotten that part.

He looks different now, of course. There was so much sweat and dirt on his face, it was hard to trace the path of the years. But there were a couple of big scars that hadn't been there before—one through his cheek, the other cutting into the corner of his lower lip. That massive, muscular body trussed up in an orange jumpsuit and shackled with heavy chains.

And those eyes, burning with desperation.

He's still Maxim, though. Still the guy I thought of as my hero. Whereas—

I go to the bathroom, take off my heavy glasses and remove the contact lenses and false eyelashes. I swipe off my heavy eyeliner, then stare at my reflection in the mirror. I look way less badass without my disguise. And these days, it's a shock to see the natural blue of my irises.

He recognized me.

With no hesitation. Not only do I look nothing like myself, but I was just a kid last time he saw me. Yet he knew me, right away.

Not possible, my rational brain tells me.

A strange feeling passes through me.… that tingle I felt when we locked eyes today.

A connection.

Like we belong together. Like all this time, we've been waiting to find our way back to each other.

I shake my head. What a stupid thought—

I have to go see him.

The thought hits me like a bolt of lightning.

I'll find the prison where he's being held, and go visit him.

It's not a smart thing to do, by a long shot. But I have to know he's okay.

My gut knots up. But if I do this, I'll expose myself to more danger. I'll probably have to show some ID. If my name gets flagged, I could be followed back to Perdue…

My thoughts churn and churn. I should get to bed.

I live alone right now, ever since my old roommate, Elinor, moved out. And that's the way I like it. I can just about make the rent by myself—it's not like I have a ton of expenses with my lifestyle—and I've got too many secrets and neuroses to share my space with someone else.

I CHECK the front door three times; check the locks on the windows, three times. Check I've turned off the stove—also three times. I never used to have OCD, never used to be so darn nervy.

I climb into bed, and pull the covers up to my chin.

I'm so sick of being scared. Of constantly looking over my shoulder. The day I went to the hairdresser's and got my hair bobbed and dyed red, some of the weight lifted from me. But it wasn't enough. The government put me in witness protection, found me a little house, a new identity. But they don't understand what my father is like, how far his reach extends. How ruthless and vengeful he is. I knew I couldn't trust them to protect me. After one of the agents handling his case disappeared in mysterious circumstances, I ran out on them.

Somehow, I found my way to Perdue Town. I've been so lucky getting the job at Sinner's, and a friend like Elinor, and this little apartment. And I've even started sleeping at night.

But now—

A full-body wave of panic goes through me.

Maxim understood right away that my disguise wasn't enough to keep me safe.

He says he's coming back for me.

But how?

Please let him be okay.

I say it over and over, like a mantra.

* * *

There's a blizzard blowing outside. Hailstones slamming against the windows. A brutal winter storm is raging…

My eyes snap open. I take in the dark ceiling of my bedroom. The silence.

There's no blizzard. It's midsummer. I was pouring in sweat today while I was serving the prisoners.

I was just having a nightmare, one of many. The

clock on my nightstand says 4:48am. It'll be getting light soon. I close my eyes again—

Tap, tap!

What was that? I jerk upright.

Tap, tap.

There it is again—something hitting the window.

Just like hailstones.

Ice shoots down my spine.

But not.

I want to pull the covers over my head and curl into a ball. So goddamn sick of being scared.

Something flips in me.

I leap out of bed and tear the curtains wide open.

And I scream as a pair of pale eyes stare back at me.

My eyelids flutter. It's still dark and I'm lying on my back. There's a smell of the outdoors and a rich masculine scent. I feel like I'm being embraced in someone's arms.

What the hell?

My eyes open wide and I let out a gasp.

There's a man's face, peering into mine. Rugged. Strong features, with a broad, angular jaw. A scar cutting across his cheek and chin. Cropped dark hair and a five o'clock shadow.

Maxim?

"Emory, it's okay. Relax," a familiar deep voice says.

Adrenaline pumping through my system, I wriggle out of his arms and pull myself upright.

"W-what are you doing here?" My head snaps to the window. It's closed, just like I left it.

"I climbed in," he says. "I'm sorry I scared you."

He's wearing a white T-shirt and bright orange pants. The lower half of a prison jumpsuit. "You broke out of jail?"

He reaches for me but I pull away. My heart is going so fast, it's making me dizzy.

"I needed to get to you."

"B-but why? How did you—?" I exhale slowly. "You were right—I am in hiding. I didn't expect anyone to recognize me."

His gaze drifts over me, and his eyes turn tender. "You've done real well. It's a good disguise, Emory. But it's not enough. They can still get to you."

I shake my head confusedly, desperate to understand. Did he follow me all the way from the chain gang? It doesn't make sense. The last I saw of him, he was being shot. "Your shoulder—" I cry.

He pushes up the sleeve of his T-shirt, and my mouth falls open. Right there, at the top of his massive shoulder, where I saw the bullet entering—where blood spattered from the wound—is a small, old-looking scar.

"I heal fast," he says.

"No one could heal that fast."

"Emory—"

I shiver. Every time he says my name, my eyes automatically lock onto his. It's like he's calling directly to my soul. Like there's an irresistible force connecting us. And I love hearing my old name, my real name on his tongue. I haven't heard it for such a long time.

Maxim's voice is tense, and I sense he's about to tell me something important.

"I'm a shapeshifter. You know what that is?"

"Tell me," I murmur, wanting him to say the words. Some layers of memory are beginning to separate out. Moments from the past—where he seemed to have fur spilling from the cuffs of his suit. Where his canines seemed longer than a man's should be.

"It means I have an animal, right here." He lays a massive hand on his chest. "I'm half-man, half-wolf. Sometimes the man is in charge, but other times, the wolf takes over. It means I'm strong. Almost impossible to kill with a bullet. And I have enhanced senses. That's how I found you here. I followed your scent."

"You followed my scent?" I echo. "All that way?" I know it's screwy that out of all the things he's just told me, this is the thing I'm hanging onto.

He nods. "I'll never leave you alone again, Emory." His light-colored eyes blaze with intensity. With… yearning?

My breath shudders in my throat. "Why? What am I to you?"

"We're connected. Don't you feel it?"

I get that tingle again. I *do*.

I study his features. Time has made his face more rugged. Now his face is no longer covered in dirt, I can see a bunch of smaller scars, too. But, to me, he's even more handsome than before.

I feel like… I want to be held in his arms. Like I want those firm lips to press to my own. Like I want to feel him deep inside me.

But he's Maxim. My childhood hero. I shouldn't feel this way about him.

"I'm going to protect you," he says. "Keep you safe."

Protect me. Okay, that's what he means. Just like he used to.

But he just broke out of jail.

"You came all this way." I indicate his bright orange pants. "Wasn't it dangerous?"

He shrugs. "It was nothing."

"But won't they come after you?"

He sighs. "They will. I was working undercover. I did a deal with the DA in exchange for my brother's freedom. He's in a shifter max-security prison."

I blink, absorbing the information. Sounds like the Maxim I knew—generous, self-sacrificing.

He reaches for my hand, and I let him take it. Electricity seems to flow between us. I used to grab onto his hand when I was a kid, wrapping all my tiny fingers around one of his huge ones. But this is different. I imagine those huge, callused hands stripping off my clothes, running all over my bare body. Touching my breasts, my—

I'm so glad he can't read my thoughts. Can't tell that there's a very inappropriate ache between my legs right now.

"You need to leave with me, now, Emory. There's someplace I can take you, that no one knows about. You'll be safe."

Safe. That sounds like heaven. And if Maxim promises I'll be safe, I believe him—

A stab of realization hits me in the gut. "Wait—you said your brother *is* in prison?"

He nods.

"So, he won't get out if you don't hold up your end of the bargain?"

"It's done."

I gasp. "Maxim! You have to go back!"

"Forget about it. I made my decision." He holds his hand up to counter any arguments. "You can live a sweet life someplace quiet," he continues. "Out in nature. Reading books." He crooks one of his thick eyebrows. "You still like reading books, right?"

"More than anything," I admit. "But I find it hard to relax these days."

That look of tenderness fills his eyes again. "I'll help you relax. Get back to your passions."

My heart thuds. Is he imagining staying with me in this secret place?

"Go pack a bag and let's get out of here."

I close my eyes and think about being with Maxim. Protected. Connected with him.

Then I think about all the danger he's going to be in if he stays with me. How his brother will be stuck in shifter max security jail, whatever that is.

"I can't," I tell him. "I have a life here. My boss needs me in the kitchen."

He stills, then shakes his head in incomprehension. "Your safety is the most important thing. Your boss can find a new employee."

I sigh. "I just can't, Maxim. I'm sick of running."

He gets to his feet with a growl of frustration, then

he paces around the room, hands laced behind his head. "That's your final answer?"

I nod. "It is."

He stops pacing and his lips quirk. "Guess I'll just have to be your personal bodyguard."

"No—!" I yelp. I didn't anticipate this. "Not happening."

He shakes his head, pretending he's sad. "It's one or the other. Your choice."

His jaw is jutting out, and he looks hard, uncompromising. There was a reason why he was my father's most senior bodyguard.

"And what if I choose to just take my chances instead?"

"No!" he barks. "Your safety is my responsibility, now, Emory."

I stare at him in awe. He's so powerful. Used to getting things his own way.

After being alone for so long, having to choose between a series of shitty options, being bossed around like this is…. refreshing.

And not only that—it's as arousing as hell. I can feel that my panties are damp and my nipples have turned to aching pebbles.

Oh, shit—and I'm only wearing this flimsy tank-top and shorts. Cheeks warming, I fold my arms across my chest. Please don't let him have noticed. He's going to think I'm a total pervert.

"What's it to be?" His voice is gentler now.

"You can be my bodyguard," I mutter.

"Good girl." He says it slow and caressing, and now I

feel like I really want to be his good girl. Hell, I want to be *his*…

My breath catches. What do I even mean by that?

I have no idea. All I know is that the way he looks at me ignites a fire inside me that's going to be near impossible to put out.

4

Maxim

I want Emory Manzoni like I've never wanted anything in my life.

I'm lying on the couch in her living room, staring up at the ceiling. It's the softest bed I've lain on in a long, long time, believe me. But I've barely slept. My animal's been churning inside me all night long.

It's chosen her…

And it's so goddamn wrong.

She's fifteen years younger than me, and she used to be my… my what? Surrogate niece? Little sister? A kid I used to protect, anyway. And I shouldn't be thinking about her like this.

But she's no longer a little kid—she's a sexy woman with ripe curves. And all I can think about is how much I want to strip her naked, bathe every inch of her body with my tongue, then plunge my cock between her sweet thighs and take her innocence.

The sight of her last night in nothing but a flimsy white tank-top and those tiny pink shorts… I'm sure she had no idea they were semi-transparent, and when she flicked her lamp on, I could see the dark shape of her pebbled nipples and the outline of her little pussy. I just about blew my load. It was all I could do to control my beast.

I'm a dirty, dirty wolf, and I'm going to hell.

My animal thinks it's found its mate at last. But she can't be mine. She's too young. And, despite the family she was born into, too innocent for a man like me.

I'm not going to notice how luscious her tits and ass are.

I'm not going to imagine how my cock would feel sliding between those sweet cherry lips of hers.

I'm going to protect her, that's all.

And I've already screwed up. I should've gotten her the hell out of here last night. Bodyguarding her is not a good idea, at all. But when she explained how important it was for her to stay in Perdue, she twisted a knife in my gut. She's finally found her people here, a shred of happiness. God knows she's had little enough happiness in her life.

Sure, I can keep her safe on the streets. Eighteen years of doing this job, and I'm the best in my profession.

But what if someone takes me out? What if the prison service catches up with me and hauls me back to jail? All the shit that went down yesterday was less than a half hour from here. It won't take a genius to follow the trail back to Perdue.

I snort out a laugh. Twenty-four hours ago, nothing would've gotten me out of prison. It was where I wanted to be. Helping my brother was the only thing that mattered. But now…

The bonds of brotherhood are unbreakable. But so is the mate bond. And she's so vulnerable. She needs my protection.

I mean what I said—I'm never leaving her alone again.

A memory drifts up from the depths:

Once she asked if I would marry her when she grew up. What a funny little thing she was. So earnest.

One day, you'll find someone your own age, I told her, trying to keep a straight face. I couldn't have known that when she reached adulthood, my animal would choose her.

Now the answer is yes.

I'd marry her in a heartbeat.

Put a ring on her finger.

Right after I'd given her my claiming mark.

There's a muffled creak. I jerk upright. Her bedroom door is opening. My wolf's ears prick up. Every part of me stands to attention. And I mean *every part*. I hunch forward so she won't notice my monster erection as she emerges.

Her auburn bob is all mussed, and she's wearing a bathrobe, and her feet are bare. Does that mean she's naked underneath it? My beast's nostrils snuffle, desperate to pick up her scent.

Her gaze shoots over to me, checking whether I'm awake. It's adorable. She's all shy now, like we are strangers again.

"Good morning," I say, keeping my voice low so I don't scare her.

"Hi." She waves self-consciously. "I'm just going to take a shower."

"Sure thing." I stretch casually, trying not to stare as she pads off.

When the bathroom door shuts, I get up—although every nerve in my body wants me to bust in the bathroom and join her in the shower.

Instead, I go through to the kitchen. It's a nice little room. There's a slatted blind at the window—that's smart. Good for providing privacy. I ease the slats apart with two fingers and peer through. There's a building directly opposite that looks kind of abandoned. Not good. If I was going to watch Emory, that's exactly where I'd hang out. I locate the coffee maker, fill it up and flick it on.

A few minutes later, the smell of good coffee fills my nostrils. I sure missed real coffee while I was in jail. Along with food that I'd hunted myself, and freedom to run. Being locked in like this has been hell for my animal. It's been starting to go a little stir crazy. I even volunteered for the chain gang, knowing that being outdoors would give it a little respite, no matter that I was chained at wrist and ankle. And thank the heavens that I made that decision. If I hadn't, I would never have come across Emory again.

I go to the fridge and see what's in there. I want to

make her breakfast, but to be honest, cooking is not my forte. I try to remember what she liked eating as a little kid. I shake my head. That was dumb. It was probably chicken nuggets and fries. As if she'd enjoy eating the same things now. She's a grown woman.

There's a click as the bathroom door opens again. A jolt of electricity goes through me, but I force myself not to turn around. She doesn't want to feel like I'm watching her. I hear her pad into the bedroom. I pour out two mugs of coffee and when I'm done, she's back again.

She's wearing a tight black V-neck shirt and tight black jeans, and she's breathtaking. Her hair is wet and tousled, like she just towel-dried it, and her eyes are huge and sparkling blue, full of the morning sunlight.

My breath catches in my throat because now they remind me of those eyes that I knew from before.

She flashes me another self-conscious smile, which connects directly with my cock. I turn my head sharply, break the eye contact. Gotta keep my beast under control.

"I just dug some things out for you," she says. Belatedly, I notice she's carrying a phone and a bundle of clothes. "This is my spare phone. The WIFI's already connected and we can get you a SIM on the way to work."

"I sure appreciate that." My girl's so smart and resourceful, I think as I unravel the clothes. There's a gray T-shirt and a pair of jeans. Both man-sized. My beast gives a bellow of jealous rage.

"You have a boyfriend?" I burst out. I'm already imagining tearing him to pieces.

She blinks. "N-no. I'm single."

My beast withdraws an inch. *An ex-boyfriend then?* I survey the clothes. They're massive—shifter-sized. She's been dating some beastly asshole who's not capable of protecting her? I'll rip his head off. Make him wish he'd never been born.

"They were lying in the closet when I moved in here," she continues. "Think they belong to some guy who was mated to a girl who used to live here."

Ohh. Someone else's boyfriend. I can stop being a jealous lunatic. I shove my animal back down.

"There's never been anyone else," she says, so quietly I almost miss it.

I go still. *Did she really just say that?*

She's a virgin, just as I thought. Untouched, since the last time I saw her.

I avoid looking her in the eye, for what she might see in my expression. But when I finally dare to fix my gaze on hers, her lower lip is trembling, but she looks… eager. *Like she really wanted me to know?*

Need pours through me like liquid fire.

Damn. I need to get out of here, before I try to seduce her.

"Thanks for the clothes." I lift my hands in a clumsy gesture. "I'll just go shower."

She closes her eyes, like she's relieved. "Bathroom's just there."

I close myself into the bathroom and lean against the door. Shit. The atmosphere in there was electric. I could barely hide my feelings from her, or keep my beast under control.

I strip off my dirty T-shirt and prison jumpsuit and jump right into the shower. The shower gel is a pink, feminine scented thing, but I squirt it into my hand and rub it over my body eagerly. I love that I'm using the shower gel she just used to cleanse her own body with.

Did she use a sponge or her hand? I wonder as I lather up my torso, then move down to my cock. Does she use her hand to wash her little pussy, her small fingers sliding between the slippery folds? Does it turn her on to touch herself like that?

Shit, my hand is pumping up and down my cock as I imagine her in here, naked, caressing her own breasts, her little pussy. I imagine she's with me now. How I'd lift her up, wrap her legs around my waist and plunge my huge, slippery cock into her tiny virgin hole.

She's mine. Every bit of me knows it.

My hand pumps faster and faster, up and down my swollen shaft. In my fantasy, I'm buried deep inside her pussy, my rough hands squeezing her lovely tits while her head is thrown back in ecstasy, crying out my name. One more pump, and I explode, shooting a rope of cum against the side of the shower cubicle. Cum that should be flooding her womb, while she comes all over my dick.

I take the showerhead and rinse down the cubicle, watching as my seed circles around the plughole and is lost to the drains.

Can't happen, Banks, I tell myself. *This thing between you and her is only gonna exist in your* fantasies. In real life you're going to protect her. That's all.

But if she ever begs me to take her, I'll be straight in there. Spreading her sweet thighs and stretching out her pussy.

5

Maxim

When I open the bathroom door, a delicious smell of cooking hits my nostrils. My mouth waters. There she is, busy at the stove, with two pans going.

I shove my hands in the pockets of some other guy's jeans and wander over.

"Smells great."

She turns to me with a pleased smile. "Nothing fancy, just eggs and bacon. But I figure there's nothing better for breakfast."

"Damn straight," I say.

"Easy over." She dumps three eggs on a plate and adds five rashers of bacon.

"Just how I like 'em."

"I know," she says.

"Huh?"

"Once we talked about how we liked our eggs."

I huff out a laugh. "We did?"

"Yup." She looks solemn. "It was a serious conversation."

My chest warms. I can't believe she's remembered all these years. I put the plates down on the table and bring the coffee cups over, too.

Everything is fantastic.

"I can't believe how good all this tastes after all the prison food," I say.

"I'll bet," she replies. "When I was cooking all the food yesterday I made a special effort, because I felt bad for all you guys eating prison chow."

My jaw drops. "You cooked all that food yourself?"

"Yes," she says, all sweet and self-conscious again, but with a hint of pride.

"I only tasted a few mouthfuls before—before all that shit went down, but it was real special, Emory. You've got talent."

"I'm happy if you think so." She sighs. "I used to dream of being a chef. Before… you know. And I love working in the kitchen at Sinner's, but most of the customers are shifters—" She blushes. "Oh, I'm sorry. I didn't mean to imply…"

I bark out a laugh. "Most shifters prefer their meat raw, with the heart still beating. And they probably complain when the flavor is ruined with sauces and spices, right?"

She bites at her bottom lip. "Yeah, pretty much."

My grin fades because now I can't stop staring at the

redness of her lower lip. The way it's so plump and pretty. I imagine drawing it into my mouth, running the tip of my tongue across it.

Stop it, Maxim.

"Your talents are wasted there," I tell her. "You should open your own place. Not a pub. A big, fancy restaurant in a big town."

A light comes into her eyes, but it's gone fast, and she shrugs.

A knife twists in my gut again. Because I know what that shrug means, and I hate it. It's too dangerous. She'll never be able to live a public life like that.

"So, tell me about the pub. Who are the staff, the customers?" I ask, desperate to distract her.

"My boss is Meredith, a bear shifter." A smile plays at her lips. "She's like my surrogate mom. She and her sister, Carolyn, take care of all the waifs and strays who come to the town to hide out. There's a dorm upstairs where a bunch of them stay. She's been real kind to me. There's a bartender—Jason—"

My beast snarls. "Who is he?" I demand between gritted teeth.

"Ohh…" she stutters, like she's confused by the intensity of my question. I don't blame her. I'm already thinking about running him out of town.

"He's a guy. He's nice. He's good at dealing with the difficult customers."

"Is he into you?" I spit the words out, my jaw aching as my canines lengthen.

She looks stunned. "No, he has a girlfriend or something."

My beast snorts. Like that would be enough to stop him from going after Emory. She's absolutely gorgeous. So ready to be claimed. He's probably been lusting after her non-stop.

"The girls from upstairs work most of the bar shifts. There's Kelly, Amber, Jennifer…"

I nod. They're no threat to either her or me. "And the customers—mainly shifters, you said?"

"Yup. It's a guys' kind of bar. Rough and ready."

My beast swells inside me. I don't like the thought of her working there, one bit.

She grabs her phone and checks the time. "Uh-oh. I'm running late."

I grab the empty plates. "I'll wash up. You get ready."

She starts to protest, then stops herself. "Oh, that'd be great actually. Takes me a minute to…" She gestures at her face.

To disguise herself, she means.

I wash up, dry the dishes, put them away. I'm just folding the dishtowel and laying it on the counter, when I hear the light sound of her footsteps behind me.

I turn around. She's almost unrecognizable.

She stops short in front of me, her face tense with suppressed emotion. "I look awful, don't I?"

A pain hits me in the chest. "What do you mean, Emory?"

"All this." She raises her arms and lets them fall again. "This… armor."

"N-no. You look great."

Her eyes turn liquid and for a second, I think she's going to cry. "It's not me." Her chest heaves and her words tumble out fast. "When you knew me—as a kid—that's who I was supposed to be. Everything since then, has been fake. My dad shaping me to his will." She barks out a laugh. "Even when I've finally escaped him, he's still influencing my appearance."

I stride over to her, and without stopping to think, I take her hands in mine. "Emory, I think you look awesome like this. Real—" I hesitate. *Beautiful? Sexy? Desirable?*

None of these words are appropriate.

"Cool," I say at last. Like a real cool, badass chick."

She goes still.

"And that's who you are," I continue.

She shakes her head miserably. "I'm really not, Maxim. All I do is run."

"That's not true. Look at the way you turned up all by yourself yesterday and served lunch to a bunch of feral prisoners."

"What could I do? The guard refused to serve you all."

I snort. "You could've dumped the food and driven the hell away. That's what most people would've done."

She sighs. "But you wouldn't have gotten fed."

A grin spreads across my face. "And that's what makes you so special, Emory. You're not only badass, but you've got a beautiful heart." I cup her face in my hands. "Most little kids are scared of me. Guess it's because I'm so big and gnarly-looking. But you never were. I remember you tottered right up to me and started swinging on my leg."

"I always felt safe with you," she breathes. "I knew

you'd protect me." Her darkened irises are looking right into mine and her lips are a little parted. I realize I've been stroking her cheeks with the pads of my thumbs.

Like I'm in a dream, I bring my head closer, tilting my jaw. I hear her breath hitch, but she doesn't pull away.

Holy hell, she has the skin of an angel. My callused fingertips are too rough to be touching it.

Fuck. What am I doing?

I jerk away from her.

"You must be late," I mutter.

She glances at the clock on the oven. "Shoot. I am." She keeps her head down while she grabs a purse from a coat peg, but I see her cheeks are an adorable shade of pink.

She wanted me to kiss her.

The thought runs through me like fire.

But that can't be right. Can it?

I KEEP my distance as I follow Emory to work. She'd attract a ton of attention if she was suddenly accompanied by a huge, scary-looking stranger. That's what I tell her, anyway. The truth is, I want to scope out the town, check out all the vulnerabilities, places where people could be hiding, watching her. So, I cling to the shadows, a hundred yards back. I told her to act natural, to forget that I'm there, and she does. Most people wouldn't manage it, but when you grow up the daughter of a crime boss, I guess it comes as second nature to be cool and collected under pressure.

She strolls along at a comfortable pace, arms swinging gently. Hips swaying. *Damn.* Her ass looks incredible in those tight jeans. Like a juicy, round peach I want to sink my teeth into.

Guilt pours through me. I've got to stop thinking these pervy thoughts about her. It's not right. And I definitely had no right to try to kiss her when she was feeling vulnerable. I'm not that guy—

Mate—my beast insists.

No. She's too young, too innocent, too perfect for me. I'm going to protect her, that's all. I'm not going to kiss her, shove my cock inside her, or claim her. Even if I wind up with blue balls for the rest of my life.

My head swivels left and right. If I was looking for suspicious characters in Perdue, I'd be spoiled for choice. Almost everyone is shady in one way or another, as befits a town of the lost. Eyes peeping between curtains, heads disappearing around corners. It's a darn minefield. The hairs on the back of my neck prickle as my wolf takes in one potential hazard after another. My beast is on high alert, adrenaline pouring through its veins. Every part of me is screaming, get Emory the hell out of here. It's almost impossible to protect her. But protect her is what I promised to do. To let her live the life she deserves, after she's been imprisoned and controlled by her father so many years.

I follow her down a side street, onto the main street, then into a network of back alleys. She slows down, giving me time to catch up with her.

Before long we're standing in front of an old pub with *Sinner's Refuge* written above the door. She strides through the front door and hesitates, her small hand hanging onto the door handle.

I speed-walk the last twenty yards and catch the door just as it's closing. There's a big bear shifter behind the bar, and as I enter the room, her gaze homes in on me.

"We're not open yet," she says, in a voice of flint.

"Meredith, this is Maxim. He's my—" Emory has slipped behind the bar and is pulling her purse off her shoulder.

We haven't discussed this part. I was so stirred up by almost kissing her, that I forgot my usual rule—always be as prepared as humanly possible.

Meredith waits silently, watching me with shrewd eyes.

"I'm her bodyguard," I tell her, sensing that only the truth will do.

"Bodyguard?" she repeats.

"That's right." I nod my head respectfully at the older shifter. "So, if it's all right with you, I'll just sit quietly in the corner, mind my own business and keep an eye on things."

Meredith's attention darts to Emory, whose eyes are wide with uncertainty.

"Is that right, Tiana?" she says.

Tiana. My angel has a new name to go with her new identity. Of course, she does.

"Yes, that's right, he's a good guy," Emory says.

"O-kay." Meredith draws out the word and I can

almost hear the cogs of her brain turning. "In that case, you get a coffee on the house. How do you like it?"

"Strong and black," I tell her, getting the feeling that I just won an important battle. I take a seat at the least obtrusive table possible.

A few minutes later, Meredith dumps my coffee in front of me. "How long have you known Tiana?" she demands.

"Nearly all her life," I say, with no hesitation. And tense as this moment is, my chest warms at the thought. "She needs me here. She's in a lot of danger."

"Figures." Meredith looks me up and down. "You look like a big strong wolf."

"I was her father's head bodyguard."

She gives a grunt of approval.

"You got anyone else who can cook for you?" I ask.

She sighs. "Not like Tiana. But people come and go a lot here. I'm lucky to have had her this long."

We exchange a look, then I head out the back to check on Emory.

And my heart just about stops. Because there she is, doing what she was meant to do. She's wearing a blue-and-white-striped apron and a chef's hat. And she's pulling things out of the fridge and laying them on the counter. She's a chef, a real chef, I think, and a fantasy pops up in my head of her running a big fancy restaurant, with a whole team of staff working for her.

There's a weird feeling in my chest—part pain, part pride for her. I make a promise, right here and now, that I'll help her get her dreams.

"Need a hand?" I say.

She whips around. She didn't hear me coming. I'm light on my feet when I need to be.

"I'm just doing salad prep," she says.

I shrug. "I'm good at chopping. I can even handle the onions if you like?" I take in her heavy eye make-up, wondering how she usually handles it.

"Oh, that would be great. I usually get in a real mess."

Truth is, I hate the sting of onions, too. But I'll be glad if I can save her the discomfort. I get her to explain how to chop up the pesky critters without screwing them up, and I get to work.

Five minutes later, my eyes are burning like hell. But in front of me is a pile of perfectly minced onion flesh.

"Oh, wow, you're real fast," Emory exclaims. Then she tilts her head and fixes me with a mock-serious look. "Didn't mean to make you cry, though."

I rub my knuckle in my eyes. "It's okay. Even tough guys cry sometimes—" I break off. "Where did *that* come from?"

She laughs. "You used to say it to me when I was crying. My dad always said tears were a sign of weakness, but you convinced me that it takes a strong person to show their emotions."

There's a prickle in my chest. The last few years have been tough. I've achieved a lot of success, but it's come at a price, and there hasn't been much time for laughing and softness. Being with Emory, though—it's like the sun coming back out, when I thought it was gone for good.

"And I stand by that—" I start to say, but a ringing

phone cuts off the end of my sentence. It's an old landline style, coming from the hallway.

"Ti, can you get that?" yells Meredith from the bar.

"Sure thing!" Emory skips out of the kitchen and heads towards the hallway. I follow her, staying at a distance, so I'm not in her line of sight.

"Sinner's refuge, this is Tiana," I hear her say. Then some music starts up and I miss the next few sentences. But then she turns toward me sharply, eyes full of worry. She's talking about me, and it's not good.

6

Emory

"Ma'am, this is the federal prison service," a ball-breaking female voice barks.

Ice shoots down my spine.

Relax, I tell myself. Maybe they just want another round of prisoner lunches. A laugh bubbles out of me, and I clap my hand over my mouth. Yup, after yesterday's debacle, I'm sure that's exactly what they want.

"Can I help you?" I say in a high, tight voice.

"Yesterday, there was an…umm… incident…" The confident tone falters. "And one of the prisoners escaped. I'm calling to ask whether you've seen him. He's unusually tall and muscular. He has a scar running across his right cheek."

Shit. I swallow hard to get rid of the lump in my throat. "W-why would we have seen him?"

"No particular reason, ma'am. We're just tracking down leads at the moment. He's an extremely dangerous individual and it's in everyone's interests that we apprehend him as soon as possible."

What does she mean by that? Do they suspect that he's here, or are they just fishing?

There's a sound behind me. I whirl around. Maxim is standing in the kitchen doorway, watching me. A hot, dizzy feeling spills through me.

He's risking so much by protecting me. His brother's freedom. His own life. I feel sick at how selfish I've been. I should've refused his help last night. Told him to leave me alone.

Sending him back to prison would be the right thing to do. Then he'll still get a chance to save his brother.

Even though my chest hurts like crazy at the thought of being apart from him.

I'm gripping the receiver so tight, my hand cramps.

He's right here. Come and pick him up.

The words are on the tip of my tongue—

"Emory."

I startle. I'm not even sure if he said my name out loud. It's more like I heard it inside my head. Like his beast called to me. My heart pounds.

He shakes his head, his glowing eyes locking onto mine.

No.

This time, I definitely heard the word inside my head. His lips didn't move.

I heard it because we're connected.

We belong together. The certainty rushes over me.

I drop the receiver back in its cradle, and I turn to him.

"We need to get out of here, don't we?"

Maxim nods and reaches for my hand.

* * *

I'm in the backseat of an SUV, speeding along the highway heading south from Perdue. Maxim is sitting beside me, and a man I met fifteen minutes ago is in the driving seat.

Things have happened at lightning speed. After I said a panicked goodbye to Meredith, Maxim led me through the rear exit of Sinner's, where an old black SUV was waiting. He introduced the blond, brutal-looking driver as Swede, and we took off. Now, Maxim is stripping off his clothes and pulling on a brand-new shirt and jeans, and I'm doing my damnedest not to look. Instead, I focus on not asking questions as the vehicle tears through the miles.

Another ten minutes pass and the driver turns off the highway, onto a dirt track. He parks up, and there, another SUV is waiting for us. Newer and shinier than the first, but again, nothing flashy.

"Come on." Maxim jumps out and opens my door for me. I hurry to follow his instructions. Normally, I'd ask what the hell's going on. But I asked him to get me out of Perdue, and that's exactly what he's doing.

This time, we climb into the front seats and leave the driver behind. The interior of this SUV is brand-new, with luxurious leather seats and high-tech controls glowing from the dashboard.

In a couple of minutes, we're back on the highway again, and heading for a turnaround. We take a right, and as a long, straight road stretches ahead of us, I literally see the tension going out of Maxim's shoulders.

Finally, he turns his searing gaze onto me.

"I'm sorry about before. I just needed to be discreet."

"Figures," I say.

He flashes a look of gratitude. "Swede is a long-time employee of mine. I asked him to come to Perdue and be on standby in case we needed him."

I nod. "What is your business?" I ask hesitantly, thinking that the last twenty-four hours have been so intense, I haven't even had the chance to find out what he's been doing all these years.

"I run my own security company," he says. "I employ five-hundred people, all over the country. Although, I've been, uh, hands-off the past few months." He gives a wry smile. "Swede has been pretty much running things while I've been locked up."

"Must've been a real tough time."

He shrugs. "I planned for it." He lays a hand on the dash. "You're safe now, Emory. This vehicle is bulletproof. The glass, the body, everything. It's got an anti-tracking device fitted and a rotating license plate."

"It's also pretty darned comfy," I say, pushing myself deeper into the soft leather seat.

"Only the best for you…" The smile drops from his face and he looks straight ahead again, like he thought that came out wrong.

I steal a glance at him. He's so goddamn sexy and confident and in control. I swoon a little bit more. He's always been my protector, my hero. But now I want more from him. And that's so crazy. He'd probably freak out if he knew what I was really thinking right now. I'm just glad I didn't make a fool of myself earlier this morning by trying to kiss him when he was comforting me.

"We going anywhere special?" I say innocently.

A laugh bursts out of him. "You always knew how to make me laugh," he says. "I was always real serious. And being, you know, your father's bodyguard, that was pretty serious as well. But you were like this little ray of sunshine that just lit me up inside."

Warmth floods through me. I love that I have this effect on him. I promise myself I'll keep looking for ways to make him smile.

"We're going to a mountain town called Wilder's Edge," he says. "I've got a cabin there that not a single person knows about it. Not even Swede, and he's the guy I trust most in the world." He frowns. "Aside from you."

My heart jolts. "You trust me?"

"Of course, Emory." He says it like it's stupidly obvious. "You've got a pure heart. You were like an angel among demons in your family compound."

Our eyes meet.

"That makes two of us," I say softly.

After a while, we leave the highway and the road starts to wind up a mountain. I feel the tension going out of my own body as well. I found some peace in Perdue, but it was still a question of when, not if, they'd come knocking. But now, I'm with Maxim. And I trust him with my life.

THE NEXT THING I KNOW, we're pulling up in front of a rustic wood cabin, in what looks like a real isolated area.

"We're here!" I say, followed by, "oh, god, I fell asleep on you, didn't I?"

I really hope I wasn't drooling or sleeping with my mouth open.

But the look Maxim gives me is tender. "You were snoozing like an angel," he says.

Angel. That word again. All my life I've felt tainted by my father's criminal empire. But Maxim sees me as pure, and I love that.

"Welcome to your new abode," he adds with jokey formality.

I bound out of the passenger-side door.

My new abode. A rustic log cabin, with two square windows at the front, a sloping roof and a little pathway, leading to a solid-looking front door.

I used to dream about living somewhere isolated like this, far from my father's clutches. A simple life, without all the luxuries that had been bought and paid for with other people's blood. I think in my dreams, it had looked something like this.

Maxim puts his hand to the door and it unlocks. A fingerprint sensor. Okay, guess it's not so rustic after all.

"Welcome," he says.

The front door has a ton of locks that whir into place when the door shuts behind us.

"I can set up your own fingerprint sensor," he tells me. "The exterior walls are heavily reinforced. There's also an invisible forcefield that extends fifty yards around the property, and I'll receive an alert if anyone breaches it."

Inside is a combination of rustic wood and modern appliances, all understatedly stylish.

There are two bedrooms, also with reinforced doors. And they're beautiful. Wooden king-size beds, with lovely wooden closets and nightstands. "I usually sleep here." He points to the one on the left. I already guessed that one was his. It has dark covers on the bed, and it's tidy, but there's something more masculine about it. I imagine him naked between the sheets. Pulling me in with him…

He shows me the bathroom. It's ultramodern, with a bathtub and shower. The kitchen is compact, but looks like it came straight out of a design magazine. He runs his hand across the counter. "Beech wood," he comments.

"Did you design all this yourself?"

"Every last detail."

I take in the trendy-looking fridge. "Where do we get groceries from?"

"From the nearby town. I usually hunt my own meat though." He turns away from the kitchen counter. "And that's everything."

I run the tip of my tongue across my lips, suddenly aware that I'm in Maxim's lair. This place he built himself; where he hunts his own food, like the big growly shifter that he is.

I'm also aware that he's staring at me, like he can't take his eyes off me.

"Let me show you around outside." He strides across the cabin and tugs the door open.

He points out the well, the solar panels on the roof. The shriveled vegetable garden that could be revived. The woodpile for the winter months.

An image pops into my mind of the two of us tucked up inside with a fire roaring in the hearth. No neighbors around. Just him and me.

I want to be *his*. The feeling that has been growing inside me all day reaches boiling point.

Not like a girlfriend, but something more.

His mate.

The word appears in my brain, just like before.

How am I going to hide my attraction to him when we're living like this?

All of a sudden, I feel nervous, out of my depth. I pass a hand across my forehead and take a staggering step.

"Emory? Are you okay?" Maxim turns to me.

"Yeah, I think I just realized—" The words die on my lips. I'm not even sure what I was planning to say, but the way he's looking at me renders me senseless.

His wolf. For the first time, I really see his animal behind his eyes. And they're no longer pale blue, but dark. Because his pupils have dilated, flooding the irises.

His attention is so intense, I feel it in my body. A drumbeat of need, connecting me to him. Energy crackling between us. Drawing us closer and closer.

He takes a half-step toward me—

7

Maxim

She's so goddamn tempting. Her lips are all red, like a perfectly ripe cherry. Her beautiful face is tilted toward me, and her cheeks are flushed.

So ready to be claimed.

"You have any idea what you're doing to me?" I blurt out.

She blinks. "What am I doing?"

A groan bursts out of me. I can't deny my passion anymore. "Driving me wild."

Her eyes get very wide. "Really?"

"But I can't." I make a final attempt to shove my wolf back down, act respectable.

"Why?"

I shake my head. "Because I used to have tea parties with you"

She breaks into a smile. "But that was a long time ago, Maxim. I'm a grown woman now."

"You sure are." I can't stop staring at her lips. I dip my head and claim them for the first time. She tastes like summer strawberries. Her mouth is so soft and small. And she's kissing me, too. She's not freaking out, but clinging to me.

The realization hits me like a thunderbolt. Her small hands are gripping the back of my head, and she's tilting her jaw, inviting me in.

She wants this as much as I do.

I don't hesitate. My beast roars inside me, and I plunge my tongue between her full cherry lips.

She gives a little moan, and her tongue dances against my own. I kiss her deeper and deeper. Our mouths meld perfectly. As if we were made for each other.

She's fifteen years younger than me, but this feels so right. She's what I've been looking for all my life. This sweet virgin is mine to claim.

"You know how much I want you?" I growl.

Her eyes are bright, lips parted. "I-I didn't know if you liked me, like—"

Like her? It's such a ridiculous notion, I laugh.

"I don't just like you. I love you, Emory," I say. It's way, way too soon for that, but it's the truth.

Her beautiful features freeze in shock. "You do?"

I nod. "I've loved you since you were small. But it's a different kind of love now."

Her breath hitches. "What kind of love is it now?" she whispers, like she hardly dares ask.

"It's fierce, passionate. Full of desire to make you mine." My voice comes out as a feral growl, but I'm not gonna apologize for it.

She makes a small sound, part gasp, part sigh, and she stares at me, her eyes bright and unblinking. "Maxim, I-I—" She breaks off.

"You don't have to say anything." I catch her hand and kiss it. "Just tell me you want me, too."

Her tongue darts out and licks her lips. "I do. I want you *so* bad."

I stare at her, hardly believing my own ears. This beautiful, stunning girl, who could have anyone, wants me, like I want her? I crush my mouth against hers again.

My beast pushes up beneath my skin. *Claim her, right now,* it roars.

She makes little whimpers as I plunge my tongue in deep. I imagine how she'll sound when I push my cock inside her.

My cock is so hard, it hurts. I need more. I need to see her naked. Need to taste her sweet body.

"Show me," I growl, against her lips.

"Huh?"

"Show me how you want me." Fire is filling my blood, my cock is threatening to blow. But I need to know I'm not forcing her. I need to see my angel come to me of her own accord.

She draws back and something passes across her face. Her chest heaves as she takes a big breath.

Then she lifts up her shirt and tears it right off her head.

I swallow hard, and take in her pert tits for the first time. She's wearing a pale pink bra. It's lacy and transparent, and I can make out the outline of her nipples. And they're hard. Aching to be taken into my mouth. While I'm still staring at them, mesmerized, she tugs at her jeans, pushing them off her hips. The scent of her arousal rises to my nostrils. A hot, fertile fragrance. She's so ripe, so ready.

Her panties are also pink lace.

"Beautiful," I growl.

She tilts her head to the side, looks shy again. "I hoped you might see them."

Holy crap. "You thought that when you got dressed this morning?"

She bites her lip. "Uh huh."

I'm dead.

A growl breaks from my throat. I can't hold back a second longer. I want to claim her right now, out here in the wild. But this angel deserves a soft bed for her first time.

I snatch her up in my arms and drag her inside, kicking the door shut behind me.

* * *

Emory

I LIE BACK on Maxim's bedsheets, trembling. A little bit from nerves, but mainly from my crazy, ridiculous need for him.

This is happening.

This guy—who I had a little-kid crush on, who's been driving me insane with lust for the past two days—is really going to be my first.

The bedroom door creaks and I hold my breath as Maxim strides in.

Massive. Brutally handsome, with his scars and hard features. His presence fills the small room, and his eyes burn with pale light as they rake over me.

I feel exposed under his gaze. My nipples have turned to aching little pebbles and I can feel that my panties are damp between my legs, but I hold still and let him look. I want to savor this moment. Remember every last thing about it.

My own gaze zeros in on his erection, which is jutting out, straining against his zipper. It's so freaking huge. I've already felt it, pressing against me, like it's been trying to find a way into me. My pussy is throbbing at the thought of it inside me, taking my virginity. But is it even going to fit inside me?

I watch his hand go to his belt. Looks like I'm about to find out.

He unfastens it, slowly. I can't breathe. Every last bit of my attention is focused on the deliberate movements of his hands. I've never even seen a cock before. I'm glad that the first one I'll see will be his.

Then he stops. And instead, he tears his shirt over his head.

And my mouth falls open. What a body. Huge, ripped, tan, and covered in scars. Knife wounds, or claw marks, it's hard to say, but they're scattered over his torso.

"C'mere," he growls, and he's on me. He catches me up in his arms and covers me with burning kisses. I run my hands all over him. His skin feels like velvet, and I can't get enough of it.

"Emory, my angel," he mutters, his mouth hot on my skin, as he kisses his way down from my mouth to the valley between my breasts. His hands, rough but skillful, are behind my back, and he strips my bra right off. My hands shoot up to cover my tits. No man has ever seen them before.

He shakes his head "Let me see them."

Obediently, I drop my hands again. Hold them down at my sides and let him look.

A sound of pure need breaks from his throat, and he falls on them. Cupping them in his strong hands, he sucks on my nipples, until I feel like he's going to eat me alive.

But he doesn't stop there. He tips me onto my back, and his rough tongue licks me all the way down my ribcage and belly, before he dives in between my thighs.

I squeak as he spreads my legs wide, making sounds of appreciation all the while. I'm so wet for him, embarrassingly wet.

"You smell so good, my angel," he mutters as his tongue dances around the edges of my panties.

I tremble. I wonder what his tongue would feel like on my bare pussy. At last, he grabs the waistband of my panties and yanks them off. I hear the fabric tear, but I don't care.

And then he's spreading me. "I want to see you, Emory," he grunts, as he pushes my thighs apart, opening me to his gaze.

I squirm and shiver under his scrutiny.

"Such a beautiful little pussy," he growls. He draws back. "Anyone ever touched this little pussy before?"

"No. Of course not," I say. I didn't know it at the time, but I've been waiting for him all these years.

"Anyone ever looked at it?"

"Nope."

"So, it's all mine."

My cheeks heat, and so does my pussy. I'm about ready to beg for him to touch me.

He goes still. "Is it mine, Emory?"

"Yes," I reply, right away, and I almost orgasm on the spot. "It's yours."

With a growl of need, he dips his head and licks me for the first time.

I let out a wild cry as his tongue slides along my slit. He feels so good, plunging his tongue deep inside me, then lapping at my clit.

He's so good, so skilled, and soon my thighs start to convulse.

"You ever come before?" he demands.

"Maybe?" I mutter.

His body jerks, and he lifts his head, keeping my thighs pinned wide apart. "Who with?"

I squirm, but his big hands are keeping me right where I am and I can't move a muscle.

"Tell me, Emory."

"Myself," I say in a small voice.

"You've been touching yourself?"

"Uh huh." My hands shoot up and cover my face.

"What were you thinking about?"

Darn. Now my cheeks are practically on fire.

"Tell me." His voice gets stern, bossy.

"You," I mumble. It's true. Ever since my hand first wandered into my panties, it was Maxim I've been thinking about. Over the years, the memory of his features got fainter, but it was always him.

I hear his breath catch. "Fuck," he groans. "Were you really?"

"Yup."

"What were you thinking about exactly?"

God, this is cringy. "Y-you stripping me naked and taking me hard."

His breathing is raspy with desire. "Tell me where."

"All over my father's house. Over the piano. On the kitchen counter. The stairs."

"Jesus, Emory. You're killing me," he says. Then a wicked look comes into his eye. "Show me. Show me what you were doing while you were thinking about having my cock inside you."

He leans back, staring at my spread pussy.

He wants me to touch myself while he watches?

Oh, god.

8

Maxim

It's the most beautiful sight I've seen in my whole life. Emory Manzoni lying back on my pillows, naked, her sweet virgin pussy spread wide open. One of her hands is caressing her perfect round tits, kneading at them, pinching her little rosebud nipples.

Fuck. I can feel my precum soaking through my jeans.

"Show me," I repeat.

Hesitantly, her other hand moves down, until it's cupping her wet, pink labia. As I watch, mesmerized, she dips a finger in her sopping little hole, then she starts to stroke her clit.

"Now tell me what you were thinking," I say. I'm

being bossy, way too demanding, but I'm not gonna stop. I can tell she likes it.

"I imagined going downstairs in the middle of the night to get a glass of water. Everyone else was asleep, but you were sitting in the kitchen in the dark. When I saw you, I startled, but you just grabbed me, and kissed me passionately—" Her voice is low and husky and her finger works faster and faster. "I was just wearing a nightshirt, nothing else, and you slid your hand underneath it, and when you realized I was naked underneath it, you just... lost control. You sat me on the kitchen table and took me...my virginity."

Her eyelids flutter closed. She's not embarrassed anymore. She's close to coming. The sweet, heady scent of her arousal is thick in my nostrils and desire roars in my veins.

"And that's how you came?"

"Mmm.. hmm... it was my favorite fantasy," she murmurs.

Darn. All this time, she was thinking of me. Something inside me unlocks.

"And now you're going to come around my cock."

Her eyes fly open. Then she breaks into a smile. "Show me," she whispers.

She watches, mesmerized, as I unfasten the button, then the zipper on my jeans, and my cock springs out from its cage. I swear it's bigger than ever before, precum dripping from the swollen head.

There's a flash of uncertainty in her eyes. I don't blame her. I'm already worried I'm gonna break her when I take her virginity.

But then she reaches for me. I close my eyes and savor the feeling of her hand closing around my cock for the first time. It's so small, velvety, and she moves it up and down with inexperienced strokes, wandering down to my balls and up to the sensitive tip.

I'm already so close. My body starts to quake. But I pull it back.

I need for my first climax to be inside her.

I ease her hand away and lay her on her back again. Then I sit back and press the head of my cock to her drenched little slit. I want to watch every moment of my dick taking Emory's virginity. I can see her tiny little opening, but she's tight. Real tight. Her pussy closes around me in a vise grip and discomfort passes across her lovely face.

"Easy, baby," I tell her. "I don't want to hurt you."

I don't want to, but it's inevitable when she's as small as she is. I withdraw, then push in again, going a little deeper each time.

She gasps and braces her hands on my shoulders. But her virgin pussy is so tight. I want her to remember this moment as something precious.

An idea comes to me. I grab her hand. "Touch yourself again," I tell her.

Hesitantly, she reaches down and starts to flick her clit with her index finger again.

Fuck, it's so darn hot watching my girl pleasure herself while I break through her maidenhead with my monster cock.

This girl, this beautiful girl is letting me take her innocence.

Her pussy walls are still gripping me tight, but in little ripples now. I force more and more of myself inside her.

She's panting, the fingers of her free hand gripping my biceps.

"Maxim, just do it," she gasps out.

And I do. One big thrust, and I break right through her virginity, my cock forcing its way deep inside her.

"Ahh!" she cries, eyes big and shocked. I've impaled her. My whole cock is buried inside her. I can feel her pussy pulsing around it. It feels hot, torn. I've got her virginity. She's mine.

But I'm still hurting her. She needs time to get used to me. I keep real still, until her thighs quit squeezing me so tight, then I pull out a little and try a small stroke.

"Fuck." Her eyelids flutter.

I go in and out, a quarter inch of a time, watching her face, tracing the signs of pleasure or pain. And then a little smile comes to her lips.

"So darn good," she murmurs.

My beast roars inside me, and I start to fuck her for real.

I plow into Emory's little pussy again and again, sliding on her wetness.

She's no longer touching herself, she's reaching for me, and I come down on top of her, holding her tight in my arms while I fuck her virginity away.

Her sweet cherry lips are parted like she's gasping for air. They're so red and vulnerable. I crush my mouth against them, plunging my tongue in deep.

And that's when she starts to tremble. I feel it all

over her, but especially around my cock. Fuck, it feels like a volcano's about to blow; like she's milking the cum out of me. Tighter and tighter spasms. And it happens. Her nails tear up my back as an orgasm rocks through her body. She thrashes and writhes as she comes all over my cock.

"Fuck, Maxim. So much better than—"

She doesn't finish the sentence, because my beast lets out a roar that echoes around the cabin, and I shoot deep inside her. Hot spurts of cum flood her little pussy, splashing her womb with my seed.

I want to breed her. To fill her belly with my pups. There'll be plenty of time for that, because she's mine. That's what matters.

My beast has claimed its mate.

9

Maxim

I could stay like this forever, lying in bed, Emory snuggled so sweetly in my arms.

But after a while, I hear her stomach rumble and I remember that I need to keep her fed.

We drive down to the nearby town of Twin Falls. It feels safer here, so isolated in the mountains, so we go together. We stop at the town's small supermarket for groceries. Usually, I hate food shopping, but it's fun with Emory. She gets excited every time she comes across some quirky ingredient. I'm adding star anise, fenugreek and pak choi to my list of things that are edible.

She's different since we mated.

No longer a virgin, my beast growls.

That's true. At the thought, my cock hardens. But it's

not just that. I hang back for a moment and watch her, skipping around the store, pausing to examine this and that.

She's more confident. More herself.

She turns her head, looking around confusedly. Then her gaze lands on me, and her features relax.

She was looking for me. Warmth pours through me.

This is how things are going to be from now on. We'll always be together. Connected body and soul.

Because she's my mate.

She's mine.

All that's missing is to give her my mark. I wanted to. Stopping my beast's canines from sinking into her flesh while I ejaculated into her sweet body cost me all I had.

But… everything happened so fast today. I don't want to do it until she's ready for it. Until she understands what it means to bear my mark.

When we're done shopping we have an early dinner at a burger bar.

"Does Twin Falls have fashion stores?" Emory asks. We're sitting side by side on high stools, gazing out at Main Street.

"I sure hope so." I'm mad at myself for not picking up her personal possessions before I snatched her away from Perdue. I should have suggested she pack some stuff in the morning, or told Swede to get into her apartment and grab some things. But I was so focused on keeping her safe.

"I'm sure there'll be something." She flashes me a

kind look, which quickly turns into mischief. "Or I can just go naked."

I almost choke on my burger. "That's a much better idea," I growl.

My mate, naked all the time. As nature intended.

"Maybe I'll make it a rule of living in the cabin."

She turns herself toward me and looks me up and down. She's still wearing her dark contacts, but I can see the heat burning in her eyes. "I like that idea," she says.

Fuck. I bite back a groan, my cock swelling against my zipper. That's why she's perfect for me. That and many other reasons.

I can hardly wait to get her home again. But first I'm gonna do my best to make sure she gets everything she needs from this little town.

We finish our food and stroll along Main Street.

. WE PARKED up at the end of Main Street, stopped at a burger bar, and now we're strolling along the sidewalk, side-by-side, looking for a clothing store

Twin Falls is a cute little town, with a café, a couple of restaurants and grocery stores. Different from Perdue. Much more open and friendly-looking.

But as usual, all my senses are on high alert, looking for the first signs of danger. Emory is watchful, too—the poor thing has probably spent her life like that. She's swinging her slender arms, gaze sweeping from side to side. But a little less than before, I think.

I want to keep her here forever, in this safe little

world where she doesn't have to look out for herself all the time. Where her fight-or-flight response isn't constantly activated. Just the two of us, living here together. I've got enough staff now that I can manage my business remotely. No one needs to see me in person. And Emory and I can live a simple life out here.

A big guy stares at Emory as we pass. My wolf snarls. A goddamn bear shifter. Even here, shifters are everywhere. I clench my fists and my animal swells inside me, ready to come out.

"Mine," I growl in an undertone.

"Not marked," he grunts.

Fury boils in me. Fur pushes up beneath my skin. Fucking prick. I'll rip him limb from limb.

"What?" Emory has gotten a couple of steps ahead of me, but she turns back. There's such an innocent, questioning look on her face. My beast retracts. The last thing she needs right now is to see me shift and tear some chunks out of this asshole.

Instead, I grit my teeth, let him pass. Dumb bear has no idea who he's dealing with.

Gotta mark her, my beast urges. *Show the whole world she's yours.*

"Oh, nothing," I tell her, taking in the soft, bare skin of her neck. The thought of marking her burns through me like fire, turning my cock rock-hard again. I'll do it soon enough. Make her understand what it means to be a wolf's mate.

"Oh, a fashion boutique!" Emory exclaims. She hurries across the street, and I go after her.

Not that I'm an expert in such things, but it looks

like a cool store. Emory seems to think so too, dashing around collecting shirts and pants and shorts.

The salesclerk is charmed by her, and she pulls out one item of clothing after another, seeking Emory's approval.

I stand in the middle of the store, arms folded, trying not to look too conspicuous. But it's a compact place and I feel like a giant. A beast in a china shop. Not only that, but the salesclerk is staring at me in a way I'm sure she thinks is subtle.

It's not. Her eyes are beady, and I can feel them scanning me from head to toe. I turn my back on her. Whatever she's thinking, I'm not interested. I pretend to be absorbed in a rack of glittery purses. Most of my attention is taken up by listening to the little sounds of Emory unzipping her pants and pulling her shirt over her head. *Damn.* I bite back a groan of need.

"How long have you and she been... you know?" comes the clerk's gossipy voice.

I open my mouth to tell her it's none of her damn business. Then I think, screw it:

"Forever," I say. Emory has been in my life *forever*.

A wave of heat goes through me as I wonder what Emory will make of that word. It seems like a long, long time before I hear the sound of the changing room curtain being dragged back. I turn around, and there she is. She's wearing her regular clothes, and her cheeks are adorably pink.

"Anything you like?" I ask, trying to sound normal. Heck, I have no idea what normal is right now. All I can think is, this girl is mine. I'm going to live with her in this little cabin, far from the rest of the world, and she's going to bear my mark on her neck and my young in her belly.

"Yup. There's a couple of things." She waves vaguely at the changing room, then swipes at her hair. She's working hard to sound normal, too, but I can smell her agitation. She's all stirred up. Because she likes what she heard? I can't wait to get her home to find out.

The clerk brings everything over to the desk and Emory rustles around under her clothes, before producing a wad of fifty-dollar bills.

"No, no." I wave it away. "Hold onto your money."

"Maxim, I have money," she insists.

I close my hand over hers. "Can you let me do this, and we can discuss it later?"

"O-kay." She shoots a glance at the clerk and gives in to me.

Good. She's starting to put her faith in me. To trust that I know what's best for her.

Later, when we're back at the cabin, I'll explain that I've already made more money than I'd ever have time to spend, and it would be a pleasure treating her to anything she wants. I'm also pretty darn sure that any bank account she's had has been frozen already.

When we get back to the parking lot, she spots a garden store, off at the far end.

I look at her questioningly.

"I was thinking it'd be nice to revive the vegetable garden," she says.

My heart jolts. She wants to stay here long enough to grow a garden together.

This is the best news.

We go in and the cheerful clerk advises us on what we can plant in the heat of summer. We pick out some seeds and a bunch of little plants. Emory is like a kid in a candy store, talking about all the salads she's going to whip up. We bring everything over to the cash desk. This time, she's too quick for me, and she pays with her secret money stash. Then she looks at me, eyes shining.

"Having fun?" I say.

"This is the best," she replies, looking twice as excited as she was in the fashion boutique. I'm so touched that she's looking forward to growing our life together.

* * *

Long, long minutes pass before we're back at the cabin again.

We chat about trivial stuff. Like how beautiful the mountains are. They *are* so goddamn beautiful they make my eyes hurt, but that's not what I'm thinking about right now, at all.

I'm thinking about her tight little pussy. How it's gonna feel stretched around my cock again. My beast is pushing up beneath my skin, its canines breaking through my jaws.

I keep busy carrying the seedlings out of the car and setting them out on the porch. The day has lost its fierce heat and it feels nice being outside now. A slight breeze blowing, the sweet scent of grass in the air.

"We home for the night now?" she asks.

"Yup." I shrug. "We've got groceries. Nothing else we need from the outside world."

"Great," she says happily. "I'll be right back."

She takes a bunch of stuff into the bathroom and I figure she'll be gone for a while, doing girl stuff. I crack open a beer and take it out onto the porch.

Perfect isolation, I think, staring out at the hazy mountains. There's not another sign of civilization in sight. We can be free out here. No need for clothes, just like she suggested. I imagine Emory being naked all the time. Ready for me.

Damn. My cock is so hard it hurts. It's tenting up the front of my pants.

Need to be inside her. Need to fill her womb with my seed again.

The front door clicks open and Emory comes out. She's gotten changed into one of her new outfits—a white tank top that clings to her tits and a pair of daisy dukes, with the little pockets hanging out the bottoms. Absolutely luscious.

Her gaze homes in on my erection. I move to change position, to hide it from her. Then I stop myself. She's my mate. I don't need to hide anything from her. Least of all my cock.

And she's not freaked out. She just keeps on looking.

"Hi." She flashes a smile as she strides over to me on her slender, bare legs.

My gaze drifts up to her face, her sparkling blue eyes. "You took off your make-up."

"Yeah." There's that shyness again. "Must be weird looking at me, with my dark eyes." She lifts a slim shoulder in a shrug. "I guess I need to stay in disguise when we're out in Twin Falls. But here, I want to be... as you remembered me."

A groan of need rolls out of me. She did this for me.

"Come here," I growl, holding my arms out. She comes to me, clambering onto my lap and straddling me.

Her pussy comes to rest against my cock, while her tits are inches from my face. She's not wearing a bra. Those hard little rosebuds are pushing at the light fabric.

She feels so darn good in my arms as I hold her tight and kiss her long and deep.

When my tongue plunges into her mouth, she starts to make little sighs and moans, then her hips move back and forth along the length of my cock.

"You ready for my cock again?" I growl.

"Mmm," she murmurs.

"This little pussy of yours isn't too sore for me?" I unzip her shorts and slide my hand into her panties.

Fuck, she's already wet. I slip a finger inside her. At first she tenses, then she lets out a sigh as I work it back and forth.

"We just need to get you warmed up, my angel," I growl. "Take those shorts off."

She slides off my lap and shucks them off, along with her panties. Then she stands there in just her tank top, biting her lip. So sexy, my girl.

I stare at her bare pussy, mesmerized. It's pink and swollen, and some of her juices are leaking down her thighs. It's gonna feel so good sliding down my cock.

When I lift my gaze again, I discover her eyes are laser-focused on my dick. Pure need shudders through me. I grab it, wrap my hand around it through my pants.

"You want to see my cock?"

"Uh huh," she says.

It's all the encouragement I need. I tear off my shirt and pull my cock out of my pants. It surges in my hand, desperate to get inside her.

She steps toward me again, and suddenly, she drops to her knees between my legs. Her auburn hair obscures my view, but something wet and very soft encircles the head of my dick. Her beautiful mouth.

Holy crap. She's sucking my cock. I don't dare move in case she stops what she's doing. Her tongue swirls around the head and she lets out a moan. Then she moves her head up and down, trying to take me in. It's a lot for her to take. I feel her jaw stretching wide to accommodate me. When my dick hits the back of her throat, she chokes a little, but she doesn't pull away. She keeps sliding in and out, trying her best to pleasure me.

"Fuck," I growl. I should hold back. But I can't resist sliding in a little deeper. One… two… three strokes. She chokes again as my dick enters her throat, but she doesn't pull away. She takes it because she's my mate; she's made for me.

I see that one of her hands is between her legs. She's touching herself. Sucking my dick is turning her on.

What a sight. It's too much. I'm gonna cum before I'm even inside her. And even though I'd love to come down her beautiful throat, I need to be inside her when I give her my mark.

And that's what's gonna happen. This time, my beast won't quit until it sinks its teeth into her tender flesh.

"Emory—" I grit out.

She lifts her head, her lips all red and shiny from tending to my cock.

"C'mere." I lift her up onto my lap again, and I penetrate her pussy with my swollen dick.

Damn, her muscles are so tight. Her fingers dig into my shoulders and her thighs tense. Discomfort chases across her features as more and more of her weight comes down on me.

But at last my cock hits home, and she gives a wild cry.

Slow at first, while her tender virgin pussy gets used to me again.

I hold her tight, kissing her deep while she learns how to ride me. Just this morning, she was a virgin, but now she knows exactly what to do. Her hips grind out a sexy rhythm, up and down, up and down, while her slippery pussy clenches around my cock, milking me. *Fuck.* So good.

She's panting. I'm going to fuck the climax out of her. I grasp her hips, and I thrust into her, faster and faster. Yet again, my beast's claiming urges rises up in me.

And suddenly, it's happening. My jaws ache as my beast's long canines push their way through.

Now.

All thought is flying out of my head as my animal

takes over. "I'm gonna give you my mark," I grit out. I lift her up and bend her over the outdoor table, just like in those dirty fantasies of hers. Then I grasp her lovely ass in my big rough hands. "So everyone will know you're mine."

I'm scared she's going to pull away, to tell me she doesn't want it. But instead, she

arches her back, spreading herself for me.

Fuck, she looks unbelievable like this, her pussy so wet and swollen, beneath the little pink rosebud of her asshole. She's still wearing her tank top, but I pull it over her head, needing her to be completely bared to me.

I'm planning to tease her a little bit first, rub my cock up and down her soaking-wet slit. But she grinds her hips, her pussy chasing my dick. When I hold still, she starts to push back on me, impaling herself on my cock. Damn, what a woman.

I can't hold back any longer. My fingers bite into her round hips, while I force my cock inside her tight virgin pussy again.

She cries out as my monster plunges into her tiny hole. The sight of my huge cock disappearing into her cunt, while her little asshole opens a little like it's begging to be claimed as well. One day, I vow, when she's ready, I'll claim every single part of her.

But now, my beast's jaws come down on the back of her neck at the exact moment that my dick hits home, buried to the hilt inside her.

My animal swells inside me.

Claim her, it roars.

My teeth bite down, while my hips pound her hard. She's so tiny, so soft, so delicate, but she takes all I've got to give. Of course, she does—she's my mate.

As my canines break through her skin, she gives a loud cry, and holy fuck, she's coming again, her pussy spasming around my cock while I give her my claiming mark.

"Fuck, feels so good!" she pants, while I screw her against the table.

I made her come, with my teeth, with my cock. And at last, my seed bursts out of me, and I feel it spurt deep inside her, joining the second load I gave her earlier.

Mine.

My angel is mine. Forever.

10

Emory

My eyes open on an unfamiliar ceiling.
Then I remember.

What a day.

And for the first time in my life, I'm not alone. I'm in Maxim's bed, snuggled in his arms. We're both naked and he's holding me tight against his huge body. What a blissful feeling.

I'm his mate.

After a night's sleep, that seems impossible. Except—

I put my fingers to the sore spot on the back of my neck. It kind of throbs when I touch it or think about it.

He gave me his claiming mark. Which means I'm his, forever.

There's also an ache between my thighs, from where

his giant cock took my virginity, and pounded me three more times that day.

Those naughty teenage fantasies I used to have about being his… they were nothing compared to the reality of being ravished by Maxim. Of coming all over his cock, while he set my insides on fire.

And my childish brain wasn't capable of imagining myself being *mated* to him.

A wolf's mate.

Maxim's mate.

I say the words over and over in my head, and tingles run through me.

This is real.

It means he'll protect me, always. We'll be together forever. One day, when I'm ready, I'll bear his pups. Last night, he explained to me what being a wolf's mate really means.

It means loyalty.

A lifelong partner bond, that nothing can break.

Being completely protected by your mate.

Frequent mating, and plenty of pups.

Maxim is ready for pups right now—his eyes turned soft as he told me. He can't wait for us to have kids. But he knows I've got a bunch of things to do first, before it's my time.

He's right—I think it'll be a couple of years before I'm ready, but I know he'll be a great father when the time comes.

Maxim's breathing is slow and regular. I lie still so I don't wake him, and I just enjoy the moment. I stare up at the wooden ceiling, just breathing, inhaling his sexy, masculine smell.

No one knows we're here. Maxim got me to ditch my phone SIM, and I've got a brand-new one. There's not a single thing that can track us to this lovely little place.

For the first time in so many years, I don't feel scared or watchful. I know I can trust him. My own professional bodyguard, whose senses are hundreds of times sharper than mine.

I'm finally safe from my father's reach.

Lying safe and protected in Maxim's embrace.

What a feeling.

At last, he gives a long, sleepy sigh. I freeze, a tiny bit of me wondering if he'll decide yesterday was all some terrible mistake.

"C'mere," he growls, and he draws me closer to him.

Little starbursts of joy fizz inside me.

"Good morning, my angel." He plants a kiss on my forehead. "How did you sleep?"

"Think I slept right through." I frown. "Wow, that's a first."

"Probably because it was real quiet out here."

"Or maybe because I was sleeping in your arms."

He gives a chuckle that sounds very unlike the Maxim I know. "I'm sure glad to hear that." He nuzzles at my neck, inhaling deeply. "God, you smell incredible. Like mayflowers. All sweet and fertile." He lifts a hand and cups my bare breast. I sigh, which turns into a moan as he gently tweaks my nipple.

Then his hand slides down between my legs. "How's that little pussy of yours?"

He's inquired about my pussy a couple of times already. I love that he worries about it. I can't lie, it hurt like crazy when he tore through my virginity, but it was worth every second of pain for his cock to be the first thing that went inside me. Even when I was a lonely teenager, touching myself all the time and thinking about him, I never used a vibrator or anything. Because in my fantasies, his cock was going to be the first thing inside me.

And it has been. Stretching me out, almost splitting me in two. But so, so good.

Making me come like crazy, until I couldn't take any more.

"It's better," I tell him.

"That's good to hear," he growls. He caresses my labia with light fingertips.

That feels so good. Right away, I start to get wet, my pussy beginning to ache for his cock. He keeps going, casually, like he's in no rush at all. Heat floods my core and I squirm under his touch.

Then he spreads my pussy open, and I'm lost.

"Fuck," I mutter. I'm open, so ready for him.

"You want me to fuck you again?" His breath is hot on my ear.

"Uh huh."

"You sure you're wet enough for my cock?"

I bite my lip. "I don't know," I lie.

He climbs on top of me and shoves my legs wide apart with his big, muscular thighs. I sense his cock, looming right above my pussy, but just out of reach. He's not touching me anymore, he's just pinning me there, spread and ready for him. Kissing my mouth, my neck, sucking on my nipples.

I make a sound of frustration. Damn. He's enjoying this. I can feel my wetness seeping out of me and dripping down onto the mattress. My pussy is aching like crazy for him.

"Maxim, I'm wet enough. Fuck me already," I exclaim.

He crooks a thick eyebrow. "Hmmm… what's the magic word?"

"Please!" I burst out. "Please fuck me."

He gives a raw sound of need, and pushes his cock against my entrance.

"So big," I pant as his big, broad head enters me.

"Your little pussy needs to get used to my girth," he grunts. "I've got to stretch it out, day after day, until it's a perfect fit for my cock. And only my cock." He forces himself in, slowly but relentlessly, until he's balls-deep inside me. I feel like he's impaled me.

"You have any idea how good your pussy feels?" He stares down at me intensely.

"Tight… I guess," I gasp out.

A wicked smile tugs at his lips. "So, so tight," he confirms. "Gripping my cock like it was made for me."

I shudder at his words. "I think it was," I say.

"That's right. Made for me," he repeats, thrusting himself into me. "Whose is it?"

"It's yours," I say, right away, and another rush of arousal surges in me.

"That's right, it's mine." He goes harder and faster. Arching over me, his big cock hammers into me, screwing me into the mattress.

I come all over his dick, one, two, three times, panting, gasping, begging for more. And he doesn't quit.

Only when I'm lying helpless, all wet and messy and sated, does he grip me tight and unleash his hot seed, deep inside me.

Maxim is as good as his word—he does stretch my pussy out, day after day. I learn that being a wolf's mate also means having a lot of outdoor sex, on the porch, in the forest. It's important for his beast to mate in its most natural environment. And I'm glad to connect with it. It's always there when we mate, right below the surface, glowing in his eyes, in the fierceness of his touch, and it's part of his wild sexiness.

I love how much he wants me. He rarely wears clothes—he says shifters usually walk around naked when there are no prudish humans to see them—and I'm treated to the sight of him gloriously naked all the time, nothing concealing that big, cock from me. Most of the time it's hard, or semi-hard, always ready to shove its way inside me.

I'm a little shyer than him, and I usually wear at least a slip dress to preserve my modesty, but it only takes a touch or a kiss from Maxim, and I'm aching for my mate to claim me again.

And when we're not fucking, we get to know each

other again. Not as bodyguard and ward, but as a wolf and his mate. My sexy older man, who's teaching me so much about life.

This little cabin and the vegetable garden outside become our whole world, and I couldn't be happier.

I spend a lot of time cooking. The kitchen is high-spec and it's a dream to cook in. Maxim buys me some extra utensils, as well as the long list of ingredients I give him. All day long, I try out new recipes, and at lunchtime and in the evening, I feed him. He's always full of compliments and helpful suggestions.

While I'm cooking up a storm in the kitchen, he runs his business remotely, at the little wooden dining table, his huge frame hunched over his laptop, right by my side. Then in the afternoons, when the sun has lost its fierce heat, we tend the garden together.

One beautiful day after another.

I love what we're building together. Every day I fall more and more deeply for him. I feel like we've always been together. I even forget that there was this long period when we weren't in each other's lives.

We're in a perfect bubble.

Except for that one thing that keeps nagging at me: his brother. Rotting in jail.

Maxim doesn't talk about him a lot, except to say that he's a real good guy, and the charges against him were bullshit. But I know he must be weighing heavily on his mind.

And I can't stop thinking that it's my fault. Maxim gave up his chance to help his brother in favor of saving me.

"You can leave me here by myself for a while, you know?" I tell him one morning. He's just come back from a run in the forest, and his eyes have that wild, intense look they always get when he's just shifted back from his wolf form.

"What?"

"If you need to go and help your brother. I'll be okay here."

"No!" he almost shouts. Still naked, he strides across the cabin, snatches me up in his arms and plants me down on the kitchen counter. "You're mine, Emory." He presses his forehead to mine. "A wolf does not leave its mate. *Ever.* You hear me?"

"I hear you," I say, startled by his fierceness.

"There was a reason why things unfolded the way they did that day."

That day. All those things that could've stopped us from meeting. He could've been in a different chain gang. Another restaurant could've agreed to supply lunch. I could've refused to deliver it. All those little happenings that conspired to enable that unlikely meeting to happen. It gives me shivers to think about it.

How easily he could've slipped through my fingers.

He strokes my hair. "I'm working on helping my brother," he tells me. "But leaving you here, unprotected, is not the answer."

* * *

That evening, a seed of an idea plants itself in my head, and I do something I haven't done for a long time—I Google my father's case.

And when I click on the first result that appears, my stomach plummets:

Head of Manzoni crime family set to walk free as witnesses alter testimony en masse

Says the news headline.

"Motherfucker," I whisper. He's done it. He's got to them all.

The trial is set to continue on Monday morning, on what is expected to be the final day of the hearing. It's believed that, unless any new evidence is uncovered at the eleventh hour, Manzoni is likely to be found not guilty of the many, many crimes with which he has been charged. Legal experts describe this as the worst travesty of justice that has ever occurred in this country.

I swallow hard to stop myself from throwing up.

Previously, my father was looking at life without parole.

The FBI read out a list of charges to me while they were convincing me to testify against him. I was in tears before they'd gotten a quarter of the way through.

I've long since emotionally detached from the reality that it's *my* father, my own flesh and blood, who's been doing these despicable things. I just feel so, so awful for his victims.

Now, every single one of them has been intimidated—or worse—into not testifying against him.

Except for one.

I close my eyes as the last few months of my life flashes through my memory. The disguises, the lying, the fear. The constant looking over my shoulder.

I've got to do this.

But there's no way I can get Maxim caught up in it.

I've got to do it alone.

It kills me to hide anything from him. But if I told him what I was planning to do, he'd stop me.

I promise myself, this is the dead last time.

THE ONLY TIME he leaves me alone is when he goes hunting. These days his beast needs a release twice a day, after it was trapped in jail for so long. So, the next morning, I wait until he's gone out, and I leave. I drive his SUV down to Twin Falls, and I buy an old car with my secret wad of cash.

I leave the SUV at the near end of Main Street, with the key fob in the wheel well. Then I take a moment to call my old contact at the FBI—right before I drive hell-for-leather back to a world I hoped I'd never see again.

11

Maxim

My beast charges back home, going at full-pelt. I'm desperate to see my girl, as always. To awaken her with a kiss. But today, there's something new in the air that makes my heart beat faster than usual.

As soon as I arrive at the cabin, I see it—my SUV is gone. Adrenaline pours through me as I dash inside, check the bedroom.

"Emory!" I bawl.

But she's not here.

My beast whines and frets.

Maybe she's gone to Twin Falls to run an errand?

That doesn't seem right. We never do anything without telling the other one about it.

I grab my phone, dial her number.

It rings out.

Damn.

I pace around the cabin.

Something's wrong. I can feel it with every nerve of my body. My beast paces inside me, scrabbling to be let out.

I call five more times.

She doesn't answer.

Maybe she went shopping and left her phone in the car? That's the only scenario that doesn't turn my blood cold.

Someone came and kidnapped her? They took my car, too? So, they would've had to have come on foot? That makes no sense at all.

She decided she doesn't want to be my mate after all?

I choke back that awful, awful thought.

I shouldn't have left her, ever. Not even to run. I should've insisted on taking her with me and carrying her on my back.

My wolf throws back its head and howls.

I've got to get to Twin Falls. Hopefully I'll find some answers there. I'll shift and run all the way there. Carry my damn clothes in my teeth.

My beast starts to force its way out, fur burning my skin, bones cracking—

My phone rings. It's an unfamiliar number.

I snatch it up.

"Maxim!"

The line is crackly, but I recognize my brother's voice.

My gut tightens. He's only allowed to call on Sundays, and always via the prison's phone service. "Travis, what's going on?" I demand.

"You're never gonna believe it… I'm free!"

My breath catches. "Are you serious?"

"Yup. I'm outdoors. Looking at the bright blue sky right now, bro. And it's beautiful."

"That's fucking awesome." I close my eyes, imagining how he must be feeling. "But what happened?"

"I have no idea! A secret deal, they told me. Highly classified. I'm supposed to stay out of sight." He's garbling in his excitement.

My thoughts spin.

There's no such thing as coincidences—one of the wiser things Emory's father told me.

"Travis, listen to me. Where are you?"

"Oh, in this random town. They dropped me off at a government safe house or something."

"You have an address? Or is there a street sign nearby?"

"Oh, wait… yup."

Hurriedly I write down the address he gives me. "I'll come for you as soon as I can," I tell him. "I've just got to deal with something urgent."

"Sure thing," he says. He knows I wouldn't put him off if it wasn't real important.

I stare at the distant mountain peaks. Travis is free. That's unbelievable news. I feel his happiness and relief like it's my own. But—

"Fuck, fuck, fuck!" I bellow into the empty cabin.

Emory brokered my brother's release. That's obvious. Which can only mean one thing: she used some kind of bargaining chip.

With a groan, I tap my phone's Internet app.

In less than thirty seconds, I understand: she's agreed to testify against her father, in return for Travis's freedom.

With no concern for her own safety.

Which means she's in a ton of danger.

My crazy, reckless, beautiful mate.

I've never loved her as much or been as mad at her as I am right now.

I grab a set of clothes from the bedroom, and I let my beast emerge.

* * *

AN HOUR LATER, I'm in my SUV. Emory did exactly what I would've done in the same situation. She left the vehicle in a prominent location, and the key fob was in the first place I looked. As frustrated with her as I am right now, love and admiration floods through me. She's so goddamn smart, my girl.

Now, to work out where she's gone. I'm guessing she's arranged to meet a contact of hers someplace anonymous. But the trial is being held in Brunswick, so I head to the town, knowing she'll be there sooner or later.

I send her a text message:

Travis is out. I'm on my way to you now, baby.

Then I set my phone to auto-dial her number every five minutes.

The first time it rings out again, but then she calls me back.

"Maxim?" Her voice is so hesitant, my heart aches. I don't want her to feel nervous about speaking to me, ever. "I've got to do this. Please don't try and stop me."

"Emory, you might as well pull over. I'll be with you soon."

She's silent for a moment. "You have no way of tracking me."

"You sure about that?" I growl.

"Yup."

Darn. She's right. I should've put a tracking app on her phone. But I didn't want to cross the line from possessive to stalker. "You gonna tell me where you're going now?"

"Nope. Because if I do, you'll come and kidnap me," she says, almost cheerfully.

She knows me too well. Knows there's nothing I wouldn't do to protect her.

"Emory, this is crazy. Do you realize that?"

"I have to do it, Maxim. I can't let my father get away with this." Her voice is quiet but firm, and once again I'm in awe of her guts.

"But you've suffered, too. So much. You're one of the victims here."

"I'm still alive, though," she mutters.

"I'm coming for you. This is as dangerous as hell. Please, tell me where you are, and I'll come pick you up, take you back home."

"Maxim, if you do that, they'll pick up your brother in minutes. You want him back in jail?"

I swallow hard. Truth is, I can't stand the thought of Travis having this little taste of freedom then being dragged back to jail. It'll kill him. But I also can't stand the thought of Emory suffering anymore.

"This is for my mom as well," she continues. "I'm pretty sure my father had her killed."

I stop breathing. Because when I was working for the Manzoni family, I developed the same suspicion.

"I have to do this, for all those people, and my mom. Please try to understand that." She releases a long sigh. "I love you so much. Trust me, every part of me wants to just turn this car around and drive straight back to you. But I couldn't live with myself if that evil asshole walks free, after intimidating or hurting all those other witnesses."

I'm silent for so long that she says, "Maxim?"

"I'm going to bring you something, okay? Something to help you with the case. When I've got it, I'll call you."

"Okay."

"You're going someplace safe, right?"

"Yes. I've been speaking to my FBI handler on an encrypted line. The meeting in a small town. The place is under heavy guard."

"Okay," I say. That gives me a measure of relief at least. "Be careful, my angel. If you feel in your gut like anything is wrong—anything at all—you get out of there. You hear me?"

"I hear you."

"And, I love you more."

* * *

It's dark by the time I pull up in front of the Manzoni family compound. A sprawling mansion surrounded by fifteen-foot walls and an electric fence. Almost impossible to breach. I park in a side street and walk over to the front entrance. Police tape crisscrosses the gates. The property is empty now. Seized by the FBI. According to an article that *Siri* read to me when I was driving, the government plans to sell it, in order to compensate the family's victims.

I listen hard. It's all quiet within. I walk a loop around the perimeter wall. There's a guard or two, probably some civilian security officers. Nothing I can't handle. I return to the front gate, shift for superior speed and agility, and I'm up in seconds. The electric fence is still activated, and it emits an angry buzz as I leap over it. Clinging to the shadows of the lavish grounds, I evade three different guards, patrolling around the property. They look professional, in decent shape, for humans at least. But they're no match for my animal.

I know all the mansion's weak points. The first thing I did when I started working there was assess them all and make sure they were suitably protected. I locate the grate that conceals an entrance to the basement. I smile. It hasn't changed since I was last here. I haul it up and drop down ten feet into the basement. It's a storage space, and at the far end of the space is a heavily-protected door, with a passcode access. Her father's major weakness was his arrogance, and I remember he wasn't too careful with his passwords. I dredge up all the numbers that used to be important to him. It only takes five tries before I hit the jackpot—the date that he reached the age of twenty-one and became head of the family business. I shake my head. At least he took the precaution of reversing the numbers.

As I creep through the house, memories blast through me. I remember the pride I felt when I first became his bodyguard. The sickening feeling when I realized how corrupt he really was. And the joy of spending time with Emory—his innocent little daughter. So pure, so full of curiosity about the world—a world I thought she'd never get to enjoy.

Well, now she's mine, and I'm going to make sure she has every pleasure that life can bring. We can travel the world together. Hike the Amazon, visit the polar bears, go see the aurora borealis. Every last thing she wants.

The kitchen door is wide open, and a heat floods to my crotch as I remember all those naughty fantasies of hers. Now they're a reality, because the adult Emory is my girl.

I take the grand staircase, two at a time. Along the corridor, onto the third story, then I locate a pulldown ladder and climb up into an attic.

It's real dusty up there. It hasn't been accessed in years. I suspect Manzoni may not even have known about it. It's not the kind of thing he would have given a damn about. There's a bunch of Emory's old toys. I remember the rocking horse, the little car she used to drive by peddling her little legs, and the tent covered in pink unicorns.

At the back, I find it—a simple wooden box. There's

something important in here. Something she needs to know about. Her mom once told me that if anything ever happened to her, I should look after it and give it to Emory when she was twenty-one. I promised her I would, and I intended to keep that promise. But when her father fired me, I had to choose between going to find the box and saying goodbye to Emory, and I chose the latter. I'll never know if I made the right decision.

The lid is locked with a heavy padlock, but I break it open with my claws.

It's packed with notebooks. Diaries, I realize. I pull out the one to the far right, heart beating faster, and leaf through to the final page. It's written in a faint, shaky scrawl.

I don't have much time left. He's killing me slowly. I accept my fate. I made my bed when I married into this evil family. I only pray that someone will look out for my little girl. I trust Maxim. He's been so good to her. But Franco never keeps his staff for long...

There are two more lines that I can't make out.

My head swims, and I sit down heavily on the floor.

The official story was that Emory's mom was sick. But it sounds like her father was... poisoning her?

I leaf through the diary impatiently.

He knows I tried to leave him

Says one, dated three months earlier.

I think it's in my food. Every time I eat, I get so dizzy and nauseous

Says another.

I close my eyes. I know Manzoni is the scum of the earth. But, his own wife!?

My beast unleashes a roar.

He killed my girl's mother. This just got a lot more personal.

I pack up the box again. Then I cast around, looking at Emory's old toys. So many sweet reminders of her childhood. Which should I take with me? Emory loved all her possessions. Despite her father's wealth, she wasn't a spoiled kid, at all. She appreciated everything that was given to her.

We can give them to our kids.

My beast bounds in joy.

Yes.

Then all these memories can have a second life. A little gray rabbit catches my eye—the gift I gave to her when I was going away. I snatch it up. It looks like it's been well-loved over the years.

I'll come back later, and collect every last one of them, I tell myself. But now I need to get to Emory.

I snap a photo of the box and send it to her.

Some evidence that should help the case. Where shall I bring it?

She replies right away:

OMG!

I'm at 1603 Sedgewell Road, outside of Brunswick. Please come quick!

Come quick? She's in danger? Adrenaline pours through me.

My phone pings again:

I miss you like crazy.

My heart leaps. *On my way to you, baby,* I type.

12

Emory

The trial winds up running for another two weeks. The new evidence I've presented needs to be examined by the prosecution and defense teams. My mom was totally open in her diaries. She detailed many of my father's crimes, including his successful attempt to poison her over a long period. When I think of everything she suffered, my heart breaks for her all over again. I'm just so, so glad she kept these records.

Due to the extreme risk to my wellbeing, it was decided that I could give evidence remotely. So, for the past two weeks, Maxim and I have been accommodated at Quantico—in what they call a 'safe-suite', but is more like a subterranean bomb shelter. At first they weren't keen to let him stay with me, but I wasn't about to take no for an answer.

He's been an amazing support.

"This is not about me," he keeps telling me. "This time will pass fast. You've got to focus on yourself."

The truth is, I couldn't have done it without him.

The FBI keeps assuring me that I'm safe, that they've taken every step to protect my anonymity, but I'm still terrified at giving evidence against my father. And the defense team is brutal. They specialize in working for the mob, and they do everything they can to discredit me.

When the live video link shuts down each day, I feel mangled. Stomach churning, tears streaming down my cheeks.

But Maxim is here for me. He waits next door, and as soon as I'm done, he rushes in and takes me into his arms. Then he kisses all my tears away.

It's been real tough for him here. He's such a sweetheart, he hasn't mentioned it once, but I can tell that his beast has been struggling. It was locked up in jail for so long, then it had a brief taste of freedom, and now this.

I figure the best thing I can do to take his mind off it is to fuck him as often as humanly possible.

Every morning, I wake him up by sliding my mouth or my pussy onto his big cock. And every evening, he takes me all over our suite.

The rooms are probably bugged, but there's not a lot we can do about it. At least we're giving the Quantico geeks a good show. And as the end of the trial approaches, I swear he's fucked me over every single surface of the room.

By the final day, I'm done giving evidence. Maxim and I sit in the suite, watching on a live feed as the prosecution presents its closing arguments.

The jury deliberates for three long hours, before they return a unanimous verdict:

They've found my father guilty of all eighty-three counts. Several of which carry mandatory life sentences.

"It's over, baby." Maxim hugs me tight as tears stream down my face. "Your father's not going to hurt you anymore."

I've done the right thing, I think, as I watch that evil man—my own flesh and blood—being led from the court in chains.

I've gotten justice for my mom, and all those other people who've suffered at his hands over the years.

Maxim holds me, until all the grief and worry has flowed out of me.

Then he draws back and looks at me thoughtfully.

"Do you have any plans for tonight?"

"Not *really?*" I say, wondering at the mischievous smile playing at his lips.

"I was thinking we could go out for dinner," he says.

"No way?" I exclaim. Then my head drops. "I think it's too dangerous. I'm just worried my dad might try to get revenge on me or something."

Maxim holds both my hands in his. "Emory I'm so sorry that you have to even speak a sentence like that.

But I have thought about that, and I've enlisted a little help from our gracious hosts."

I shake my head in confusion. "What do you mean?"

"Open the closet," he says.

I dash over to it. Inside is a dress that wasn't there twenty-four hours ago. I pull it out. It's a beautiful black cocktail dress, strapless, slinky, with the label still attached. "Wow, this is gorgeous," I breathe. "And it's my size. When did you—? How?"

He grins. "I have my ways."

"Now, we're going to get ready, then we're going to take a helicopter from Quantico to a private dining room in one of Washington's most exclusive restaurants. I've been advised that it's the preferred venue for high-value guests. It's the place where the president likes to entertain his more vulnerable heads of state when they visit. The staff are highly vetted, everything reinforced, bullet-proof walls, windows, that kind of thing. How does that sound?"

I throw my arms around him, stomach full of butterflies. "That sounds incredible," I say. "Thank you so much for organizing all this. I just can't believe it."

He grins. "Well, believe it when you see it. Now, go get ready. There's a bunch of toiletries and stuff in the bathroom, too." He pulls me close for one more kiss.

My gorgeous, incredible mate.

My head swims as we lose ourselves in each other again.

"Now go." He swats my ass. "We've got a helicopter waiting."

In the bathroom, I shower with a bunch of very

fancy toiletries, then I look at myself in the mirror. I'm going to skip the glasses, and contacts tonight. And heavy make-up, and false eyelashes. I also remove the stud in my nose and all my earrings. I haven't refreshed my fake tattoos since we've been here, and a good scrub with a flannel gets rid of the final traces. The only mark remaining on my skin is the one that Maxim gave me. And I would never want to be without that one. It still tingles every time I touch it, or even think about it.

This red hair looks too much without the dramatic eyes, so I pull it back into a simple chignon, and opt for a simple coat of mascara and a slick of lip-gloss.

There. Now I look like myself again.

I slather jasmine scented body lotion all over my arms and legs, then I pull on the dress. It's body-con style and it fits me like a sheath, pushing my tits up and together, and hugging my ass.

At last, I emerge from the bathroom in a cloud of steam. And my jaw drops.

Because Maxim is wearing a tux.

A freaking tux. There's something about his wild masculinity being contained within this sharp, formal attire that's just… *wow*.

A groan of need escapes my lips, my pussy already starting to ache.

"Emory," Maxim breathes. "You look so, so beautiful." He strides over to me and kisses me carefully on the lips.

"It's okay, I'm only wearing lip-gloss."

He cups my face in his big, calloused hands. "I was worried if I keep kissing you, we won't make it out of here at all," he growls. Then he pulls away and presents me with a shoebox. I open it and find a beautiful pair of Jimmy Choo's inside, also in my size.

"Oh my god, I love them," I breathe.

"You sure?" He looks worried. "I wasn't sure if it was your style."

"Yup. Very much my style!" I brace my hands on his shoulders as I step into them. I feel like Cinderella, rescued from my evil family by my very own Prince Charming.

When we leave the suite, an FBI agent is waiting by the door. He ushers us along the corridor, up a flight of stairs, through an external door and there's a helicopter, its propellers already whirring.

Maxim takes my hand and leads me in, and in a moment, we're way up in the air, Washington's stately buildings spanning out beneath us.

It's just past sunset and the view is breathtaking, but it's nothing compared to the sight of my gorgeous mate beside me, looking so sharp in his tux. He even trimmed his beard and combed his hair for the occasion. To be honest, I prefer him in jeans and a T-shirt—or better yet, nothing at all. But it's sure nice to see him like this for one special night.

We fly over the city in a sweeping arc.

"The scenic route, so you can enjoy the view," Maxim says.

Finally, we land on the roof of a tall building. Inside is a beautiful room, done out in a cool, contemporary style. The space is big enough to accommodate maybe fifty people, but a single table has been set up right by the windows.

"We've got it all to ourselves."

Maxim raises my hand to his lips. "So, you can relax and enjoy the evening, just like you deserve."

It's all so romantic. All the dreams I never dared entertain.

Maxim leaves me over to the table and helps me to my seat. A door opens on the far side of the room, and a familiar brutal-looking blond man appears.

"Swede?" I say, uncertainly.

He gives a solemn nod. "Good to see you again, Emory. I'll be your server tonight." There's a mischievous quirk to his lips as he says the last part.

Maxim claps him on the shoulder. "I talked him into filling in tonight, since he's the guy I trust more than anyone."

Swede brings a bottle of champagne for us and pours out two glasses, then hands us each a menu. For such a big guy, he has a deft touch, and he serves us as unobtrusively as any professional server.

"To you, Emory." Maxim raises his glass. His eyes are fixated on mine, and I see so much love and admiration there, it brings a lump to my throat.

"No, to *us*," I insist.

The menu is incredible. French haute cuisine. Every mouthful more delicious than the last.

"I dream of being able to cook like this," I say, swallowing a delicious forkful of something exquisite.

Maxim takes my hand. "Emory, your wish is my command. I loved all the food you cooked for us in the cabin. But you know, it also made me sad, because I knew you weren't getting to make the most of your talents. You want to learn French-style cooking, I'll find the best teacher I can for you."

"I would really love that," I reply.

When we're finished, the helicopter is waiting for us again, and it carries us up, through a clear, starry Washington night.

I thought I'd never want to see the hospitality suite again. But I was wrong. Turns out I can't wait to get back there and tear off Maxim's perfect tux. All evening, I've been aching for him.

We've barely been in the room two minutes before we're both naked, and I'm lying on the bed, thighs spread wide, while Maxim is arching over me, his monster cock reminding me who I belong to. Bliss.

13

Maxim

We pull up in front of a squat gray house, halfway along a quiet street. My gorgeous mate is beside me, and my beast is bounding in scrabbling in anticipation.

"Ready?" I ask.

"Can't wait!" She leaps out of the car and grabs my hand.

We walk along the pathway. The front door opens and a familiar, tall, broad-shouldered figure steps out.

"Maxim!" A grin spreads across his face.

"Travis!" I yell at the same moment. We fall into each other's arms, and hug and growl and slap each other's backs, like the two beasts we are.

I draw back and look into the face I haven't seen for five years. He's been through a lot, probably more than I know, but he looks the same as ever. My happy-go-lucky kid brother, with his unfortunate habit of being in the wrong place at the wrong time.

"Am I glad to see you," he says. He turns to Emory. "And you're the one who got me out of jail. I owe you my life."

"I had a little bit of help," she says modestly.

He goes to shake her hand, but then he pulls her into a hug instead.

My beast stays calm. He's my brother and I can see the claiming mark sitting up high on the back of her neck, showing every shifter in the world that she's mine.

We go inside and start catching up on the years, and I fill Travis in on everything that's happened this last couple of weeks. Later in the evening, one of the agents brings us beer and pizza, and the conversation turns to our plans for the future. We get loud and excitable, and I can tell that Travis and Emory like each other a lot.

"She's amazing," he says as we head off to bed at last. "You're lucky to have her, big guy."

"Oh, I know," I tell him.

* * *

THE NEXT EVENING, I leave Emory in the care of Travis, and the agents who are guarding the property, and Swede, of course—who is set up with a sniper rifle on the roof of the house opposite—and I go to run an errand.

I've learned that another condition that Emory

demanded from the FBI was that her father would be sent to a shifter prison—ironically enough, the prison where Travis had been held. She's so darn smart. She got all her father's resourcefulness and quick thinking, with none of his evil. This means he won't have a single ally in there, and it should guarantee her safety, but I just want to be real sure.

When I arrive, Manzoni is already there, shackled to a metal desk. He blinks at me from behind a thick glass partition.

"Who are you… Didn't you work for me once?"

"I was your bodyguard," I confirm. "Then you fired me. Because I was making your daughter's life more bearable. Isn't that right?"

Recognition passes across his sharp features, followed by a cruel look. "Sounds about right."

My beast swells inside me. I long to rip his nasty head off.

He frowns. "What are you doing here?"

"Oh, I came to ask for your blessing."

"My blessing? What?"

"Emory and I are together. She's mine. My wife," I tell him since he doesn't understand the concept of mates.

His face transforms with fury. "No. She was meant for someone else."

I slouch back in my chair. "One of your criminal associates, right?"

He curls his lip.

"Well, don't you worry. I'll be taking good care of her. I'm gonna make sure every day of her life is filled with as much happiness as she can stand. All the happiness she missed out on when she was a child."

He snarls. "Is that why you came here? To gloat about deflowering my daughter?"

A smile tugs at my lips. "No, actually. I came to warn you."

"Warn me what?" He's leaning forward now, handcuffs clanking as he crunches his knuckles.

I sit closer, until my face is practically touching the glass, and I stare deep into his eyes. My wolf rises to the surface, and I see him flinch. He has a hard time looking it in the eye. "You're going to prison for the rest of your life. And it occurred to me that you might try to take it out on Emory in some way. But if you ever do that, if anything happens to her, I have associates at the prison who will destroy you. Eat you alive." My wolf's canines are pushing through. I let them come, and I snap my jaws at him. "And I don't mean that figuratively. You know what kind of place you're going to be kept in? It's a shifter prison. Full of hungry beasts.

"This is not an idle threat, Manzoni. You understand me?"

His face contorts. He's still not used to taking orders. But he'll learn.

"Let me hear you say it."

He snarls. "I won't do anything to hurt Emory."

"Or anyone she's connected with."

"Or anyone she's connected with," he spits.

"You should be very proud of your daughter. She's an incredible woman," I say. "Enjoy the rest of your life."

I get up and leave him still sitting at the table, trembling with impotent rage.

Then I push the speed limit all the way back to my beautiful mate, excited to give her the news: for the first time in her life, she's free. She can do whatever the hell she wants.

As long as that involves spending every day of her life with me.

EPILOGUE

Three months later

I pull up in front of our little cabin in Wilder's Edge and leap out, looking around for Emory. My wolf is tearing up my skin and there's a heavy ache in my chest that I know won't quit until she's back in my arms again. It's the same every time we're apart. There's a powerful bond connecting our souls, and it's only growing stronger, day by beautiful day.

When I left to run an errand a half hour ago, Emory was sitting on the porch, drinking coffee, but now she's nowhere to be seen.

My heart rate skips up as I dash around the building.

There she is—on the far side of the cabin, working at the vegetable garden. Crouching down, her blonde head dipped, my mark exposed on the back of her neck.

I snort, shake my head. *Take it easy, Banks.* I never stop worrying about her when she's not right by my side. I'm not sure if I ever will. Guess it's my job to worry about my mate—and make sure she's as relaxed and happy as she can be.

She turns her head, curiously. And when she catches sight of me, a beautiful smile spreads across her face. She springs up and runs to me, arms outstretched, blonde hair flying.

I hug her tight, and as our hearts press together, that ache in my chest eases away. We've talked about it before. She says she feels it, too, when we're separated. My beast settles in me, happy to be back with its mate.

But I sense something isn't right with her. I draw back and gaze into her sky-blue eyes. My pulse speeds up again.

"Emory, what is it?"

"Oh, I was just feeling sad that all the vegetables are done for the season. I loved planting this garden with you."

I grin, falling in love with her even more. After all she's been through, her spirit hasn't changed—she hasn't gotten jaded or cynical. She has the purest heart of anyone I know.

"Me too, my angel," I say. These three months have been magical. Just Emory and me in this wild little place, living a simple life; getting to know each other, loving each other more every day. I catch her hands in mine. "But, guess what? We can plant it every single year if you want."

She beams. "Yes, please. I'd love that."

"I've got something that'll cheer you up." I pull a bunch of papers out of my back pocket. "Since it's the down season for our garden, I was thinking it might be a good time to take a little trip."

I hand the papers to her, and watch in anticipation as she rifles through them.

"Two first-class tickets to Paris… and a voucher for Le Cordon Bleu cookery school…" She lets out a gasp and throws her arms around me. "Maxim! Oh, my god!"

I hug her tight. "What do you think? We need to reserve the course two weeks in advance, but otherwise, we can go any time you like."

"I think…" She draws back, tears pooling in her eyes. "This is the best thing ever. And I can't wait to go. Thank you so much!"

Warmth pours through me. She's even more excited than I thought she'd be. "This little place will always be here for us when we get back."

She nods, eyes shining. "Oh, I know." Then her forehead furrows. "I thought you said shifters and airplanes go together like peanut butter and gravy?"

I kiss her on the nose. "I might have. But I can make an exception for you."

It's true—shifters hate flying. Even that helicopter ride shook my beast up no end. But it'll have to suck it up. I'm so ready for our adventure—to see my beautiful mate exploring the world at last. Nothing could make me happier.

EPILOGUE

Three years later

"Chef?"

I turn my head, locating the voice of my head waiter, Lucia. She's at the service hatch, waving to get my attention.

"Table twenty-one wants to thank you for their meal," she calls. She rolls her eyes and grins at the same time. The compliments have been coming so thick and fast tonight, we can barely keep up.

"Thanks, Lu." I scan the kitchen. We're almost done for the evening, and my team looks to have everything under control. We've been debuting a brand-new menu, and everyone has done so well. I couldn't be more proud of my chefs.

I give a happy sigh, pull off my hat and follow Lucia into the dining room.

There's only one customer at table twenty-one. A big, broad-shouldered man with dark hair, a ruggedly handsome face, and the most incredible blue eyes.

My heart bounds. "What are you doing here?" I exclaim, dashing over.

Maxim gets up and kisses me way more discreetly than usual. He's wearing a dark suit and a light-blue button-down, and he looks absolutely gorgeous. "I wasn't about to miss your big night."

I fix him with a stern look. "I thought you had a meeting with Travis tonight?"

He shrugs. "I knew you'd be nervous if you realized I was out here."

I break into a grin. "You know me too well."

"No such thing as too well." He catches my hand and kisses it.

"So…?" I demand, my heart beating faster.

"Sensational." He shakes his head. "Every single dish was a knockout. The duck rillettes, the tartare. You've totally surpassed yourself, Emory."

"Really?" I lay a hand on my chest and close my eyes. Maxim's opinion is more important to me than anyone else's. My restaurant is two years old, and we're already won a bunch of accolades. We're currently in the running for a Michelin star, and I'm hoping this menu will seal our reputation.

"Thank you for knowing I actually, secretly wanted you here," I say, and suddenly, I'm blinking back tears. I couldn't have done any of this without him.

He wipes at a make-up smudge beneath my eye with the pad of his thumb. "I wouldn't have missed it for anything. Now go. I'm sure you've got a ton of things to do. I'll be right here when you're done."

* * *

WHEN THE LAST customers have left, I lock the doors and we have a little party for the team to thank them for being so awesome.

Maxim insists on helping, so I put him in charge of pouring the Champagne. He's the perfect host—confident and charming—and I'm so dang proud of him.

After an hour or so, the party is going strong. It's great to see my crew relax and let their hair down after an intense period of preparation. When my sous chef busts out the karaoke machine, I decide our work is done. Maxim and I sneak out and climb into his SUV.

It's always late when I finish, but Maxim has adjusted his schedule to mine, so we get to spend quality time together. He insists on picking me up every single day, and driving me home.

The last three years have been a whirlwind—traveling the world together, then setting up the restaurant. I've been real busy, but I've made sure to hire people I trust, so I get to spend plenty of time with my mate. I've just promoted the most talented chef in my team to Head Chef, so I can step back from the day-to-day operations.

When we get home, Maxim slips my jacket off my shoulders. "Are you hungry?"

"No, I'm good. I snacked all night."

"Are you tired?"

I purse my lips. "No… think I got my second wind."

He pulls me in for a kiss. "Go get showered then," he growls against my lips.

A tingle goes through me. I know what that growl means.

"Oh, I think I'm gonna go read in bed," I tease him.

His big hands grip my ass more tightly. "Not a chance."

"And why's that?" I ask innocently.

"Because I'm planning to fuck you senseless."

My breath catches. No matter how many times we've mated—and we've mated *a lot*—every time feels like the first time with Maxim.

I go upstairs and hit the shower. I go as fast as I can, yearning for my mate building and building in me.

I dry off quickly, hang up the towel, then exit our ensuite naked—just how Maxim likes me. My hair is loose around my shoulders, skimming my nipples. And the only jewelry I'm wearing is a gold ring on my left hand, to signal to the human world that I'm taken.

He's on the bed, waiting for me. Kneeling, his cock jutting out between his muscular thighs, and fire burning in his eyes. My knees go weak. At work, I'm the boss. But when I get home every night, I'm *his*. All I want is to be possessed by my big, sexy mate and his monster cock.

As he takes me in, his cock gets even bigger.

"Beautiful," he growls, like it's the first time he's seen me naked. "Come here." He holds his arms out, and I come to him.

His kiss is fiercer than usual, his hands moving

hungrily all over my body. He nuzzles the crook of my neck and inhales deeply. "You know you're fertile right now?" he growls.

I go still. "I am?"

"Very much so." He draws back and takes my hands, gazing deep into my eyes. "You know what else I'm gonna do tonight?"

I shake my head.

"Impregnate you."

I gasp. The word pours through me like a drug, filling me with longing.

"We're going to make a baby tonight, my angel."

My heart pitter patters. I'm so excited I could burst. We've talked about it a bunch, of course. How I wanted to achieve my restaurant dream before I bore our first child. It's been so hard to hold back all these years, especially when his animal has wanted nothing more than to impregnate me.

And now it's finally the right time for us both.

Maxim lays me back on the snowy white comforter than covers our king-size bed. "I'm going to fill you with as much cum as your little pussy can take." He presses his lips to my stomach, planting kisses all over it. "Until it's spilling out of you. And soon, this beautiful belly is going to swell with my seed. And you're going to be the most gorgeous pregnant mama in the world."

By now, his mouth has moved down to the little curve beside my hip.

"But first I'm going to check you're wet enough for my cock."

He pushes my thighs apart and licks my slit.

I let out a ragged groan. Of course, I'm already wet enough for him.

But he's determined to taste me. He plunges his tongue inside me, before latching onto my aching clit. He knows my body so well, how to drive me crazy, to bring me to the brink of ecstasy and back again.

The moment my thighs start to tremble, he pulls away, grasps his cock in his hand.

Slowly, reverently, he presses it to my entrance.

Like always, there's that big push. That moment when it feels like it's gonna be too much. But then he's in, stretching me out until he hits home. My pussy throbs around his huge cock, trying to accommodate it.

He laces his fingers into mine and stares deep into my eyes. "You're so sexy, so fertile," he says, in between thrusts. "We're gonna make a beautiful baby."

It's hypnotic, intoxicating.

I start to clench around him, tighter and tighter, and then I explode. Spasming around his thick rod, again and again. Milking it. Urging my mate to impregnate me. His mark burns on the back of my neck, while his thrusts get fiercer and fiercer.

"Now!" he roars at last. I bury my face in his shoulder, clinging to him, savoring the moment when his hot seed explodes inside me like a firehose, splashing all over my womb.

"Did it work?" I ask, minutes later.

He's lying behind me now, spooning me, his hand resting protectively on my belly. "Oh, yeah," he drawls.

I twist my head around to look at him.

He grins. "We're having four, at least."

I crook an eyebrow. "Guess our work is done then. We don't need to have any more sex."

He growls and slips his hand between my legs. "Not a chance. You're gonna be so sexy when you're pregnant. Your belly swelling with my cub growing inside you. I won't be able to keep my hands off you."

"What about when I get all those weird cravings, and demand foot rubs all the time?"

"That's the part I'm looking forward to the most."

I sigh happily. I think I'm going to enjoy being pregnant with Maxim's baby. Or babies.

THE END

READ THE OTHER BOOKS IN THE SERIES

If you like steamy insta-love romance, featuring obsessed, growly heroes who'll do anything for their mates, check out the rest of the books in my Obsessed Mates series. All books are standalone and can be read in any order.

Continue the series at arianahawkes.com/obsessed-mates

READ MY OBSESSED MOUNTAIN MATES SERIES

If you like fated-mate romances, with plenty of V-card fun and tons of feels, check out my Obsessed Mountain Mates series. All books are standalone and can be read in any order.

Get started at arianahawkes.com/obsessed-mountain-mates

READ THE REST OF MY CATALOGUE

MateMatch Outcasts: a matchmaking agency for beasts, and the women tough enough to love them.

★★★★★ "A super **exciting, funny, thrilling, suspenseful and steamy shifter romance series**. The characters jump right off the page!"

★★★★★ "**Absolutely Freaking Fantastic**. I loved every single word of this story. It is so full of **exciting twists that will keep you guessing until the very end** of this book. I can't wait to see what might happen next in this series."

Ragtown is a small former ghost town in the mountains, populated by outcast shifters. It's a secretive place, closed-off to the outside world - until someone sets up a secret mail-order bride service that introduces women looking for their mates.

Get started at arianahawkes.com/matematch-outcasts

MY OTHER MATCHMAKING SERIES

My bestselling *Shiftr: Swipe Left For Love* series features Shiftr, the secret dating app that brings curvy girls and sexy shifters their perfect match! Fifteen books of totally bingeworthy reading — and my readers tell me that Shiftr is their favorite app ever! ;-) Get started at arianahawkes.com/shiftr

★★★★★ "**Shiftr is one of my all-time favorite series**! The stories are funny, sweet, exciting, and scorching hot! And they will **keep you glued to the pages**!"

★★★★★ "**I wish I had access to this app**! Come on, someone download it for me!"

Get started at arianahawkes.com/shiftr

CONNECT WITH ME

If you'd like to be notified about new releases, giveaways and special promotions, you can sign up to my mailing list at arianahawkes.com/mailinglist. You can also follow me on BookBub and Amazon at:

bookbub.com/authors/ariana-hawkes
amazon.com/author/arianahawkes

Thanks again for reading – and for all your support!

Yours,
Ariana

* * *

USA Today bestselling author Ariana Hawkes writes spicy romantic stories with lovable characters, plenty of suspense, and a whole lot of laughs. She told her first story at the age of four, and has been writing ever since, for both work and pleasure. She lives in Massachusetts with her husband and two huskies.

www.arianahawkes.com

GET TWO FREE BOOKS

Join my mailing list and get two free books.

Once Bitten Twice Smitten

A 4.5-star rated, comedy romance featuring one kickass roller derby chick, two scorching-hot Alphas, and the naughty nip that changed their lives forever.

Lost To The Bear

He can't remember who he is. Until he meets the woman he'll never forget.

Get your free books at arianahawkes.com/freebook

READING GUIDE TO ALL OF MY BOOKS

Obsessed Mates

Her River God Wolf

Her Biker Wolf

Her Alpha Neighbor Wolf

Her Bad Boy Trucker Wolf

Her Second Chance Wolf

Her Convict Wolf

Obsessed Mountain Mates

Driven Wild By The Grizzly

Snowed In With The Grizzly

Chosen By The Grizzly

Off-Limits To The Grizzly

Shifter Dating App Romances

Shiftr: Swipe Left for Love 1: Lauren

Shiftr: Swipe Left for Love 2: Dina

Shiftr: Swipe Left for Love 3: Kristin

Shiftr: Swipe Left for Love 4: Melissa

Shiftr: Swipe Left for Love 5: Andrea

Shiftr: Swipe Left for Love 6: Lori

Shiftr: Swipe Left for Love 7: Adaira

Shiftr: Swipe Left for Love 8: Timo

Shiftr: Swipe Left for Love 9: Jessica

Shiftr: Swipe Left for Love 10: Ryzard

Shiftr: Swipe Left for Love 11: Nash

Shiftr: Swipe Left for Love 12: Olsen

Shiftr: Swipe Left for Love 13: Frankie

Shiftr: Swipe Left for Love 14: Niall

Shiftr: Swipe Left for Love 15: Dalton

MateMatch Outcasts

Grizzly Mate

Protector Mate

Rebel Mate

Monster Mate

Dragon Mate

Wild Mate

In Dragn Protection

Ethereal King

Boreas Reborn

Wounded Wings

Broken Hill Bears

Bear In The Rough

Bare Knuckle Bear

Bear Cuffs

Standalone releases

Tiger's Territory

Shifter Holiday Romances

Bear My Holiday Hero

Ultimate Bear Christmas Magic Boxed Set Vol. 1

Ultimate Bear Christmas Magic Boxed Set Vol. 2